# THE TRIUMPH OF LOVE

She was thoughtful as she took off her clothes and climbed into bed.

Who would have believed that so many incredible things could have happened in such a short time? It was only three days since she had fled her stepfather's house, yet it seemed like a lifetime.

Selina had met the Marquis and already she could not imagine the world without him.

He was amazingly unlike the dashing lover she had imagined might carry her off.

For one thing, he was a bit older than the man in her romantic dreams, but his sweet temper, his quiet charm and perfect kindly courtesy had enchanted her, as the brash manners of younger men never did and he had now come to mean everything to her.

What did she mean to him? she wondered.

Nothing probably.

He regarded her as a child that he was humouring.

How very quick he had been to assure her that his behaviour would be entirely proper! Of course, she would not wish it any other way, she assured herself.

But it was sad that he seemed to find the promise so easy to keep.

After all, would one little improper advance be so terrible?

# THE BARBARA CARTLAND PINK COLLECTION

Titles in this series

1. The Cross Of Love
2. Love In The Highlands
3. Love Finds The Way
4. The Castle Of Love
5. Love Is Triumphant
6. Stars In The Sky
7. The Ship Of Love
8. A Dangerous Disguise
9. Love Became Theirs
10. Love Drives In
11. Sailing To Love
12. The Star Of Love
13. Music Is The Soul Of Love
14. Love In The East
15. Theirs To Eternity
16. A Paradise On Earth
17. Love Wins In Berlin
18. In Search Of Love
19. Love Rescues Rosanna
20. A Heart In Heaven
21. The House Of Happiness
22. Royalty Defeated By Love
23. The White Witch
24. They Sought Love
25. Love Is The Reason For Living
26. They Found Their Way To Heaven
27. Learning To Love
28. Journey To Happiness
29. A Kiss In The Desert
30. The Heart Of Love
31. The Richness Of Love
32. For Ever And Ever
33. An Unexpected Love
34. Saved By An Angel
35. Touching The Stars
36. Seeking Love
37. Journey To Love
38. The Importance Of Love
39. Love By The Lake
40. A Dream Come True
41. The King Without A Heart
42. The Waters Of Love
43. Danger To The Duke
44. A Perfect Way To Heaven
45. Follow Your Heart
46. In Hiding
47. Rivals For Love
48. A Kiss From The Heart
49. Lovers In London
50. This Way To Heaven
51. A Princess Prays
52. Mine For Ever
53. The Earl's Revenge
54. Love At The Tower
55. Ruled By Love
56. Love Came From Heaven
57. Love And Apollo
58. The Keys Of Love
59. A Castle Of Dreams
60. A Battle Of Brains
61. A Change Of Hearts
62. It Is Love
63. The Triumph Of Love

# THE TRIUMPH OF LOVE

# BARBARA CARTLAND

Barbaracartland.com Ltd

# THE BARBARA CARTLAND PINK COLLECTION

Barbara Cartland was the most prolific bestselling author in the history of the world. She was frequently in the Guinness Book of Records for writing more books in a year than any other living author. In fact her most amazing literary feat was when her publishers asked for more Barbara Cartland romances, she doubled her output from 10 books a year to over 20 books a year, when she was 77.

She went on writing continuously at this rate for 20 years and wrote her last book at the age of 97, thus completing 400 books between the ages of 77 and 97.

Her publishers finally could not keep up with this phenomenal output, so at her death she left 160 unpublished manuscripts, something again that no other author has ever achieved.

Now the exciting news is that these 160 original unpublished Barbara Cartland books are already being published and by Barbaracartland.com exclusively on the internet, as the international web is the best possible way of reaching so many Barbara Cartland readers around the world.

The 160 books are published monthly and will be numbered in sequence.

The series is called the Pink Collection as a tribute to Barbara Cartland whose favourite colour was pink and it became very much her trademark over the years.

The Barbara Cartland Pink Collection is published only on the internet. Log on to www.barbaracartland.com to find out how you can purchase the books monthly as they are published, and take out a subscription that will ensure that all subsequent editions are delivered to you by mail order to your home.

**NEW**

Barbaracartland.com is proud to announce the publication of ten new Audio Books for the first time as CDs. They are favourite Barbara Cartland stories read by well-known actors and actresses and each story extends to 4 or 5 CDs. The Audio Books are as follows:

| | |
|---|---|
| The Patient Bridegroom | The Passion and the Flower |
| A Challenge of Hearts | Little White Doves of Love |
| A Train to Love | The Prince and the Pekinese |
| The Unbroken Dream | A King in Love |
| The Cruel Count | A Sign of Love |

More Audio Books will be published in the future and the above titles can be purchased by logging on to the website www.barbaracartland.com or please write to the address below.

If you do not have access to a computer, you can write for information about the Barbara Cartland Pink Collection and the Barbara Cartland Audio Books to the following address:

Barbara Cartland.com Ltd., Camfield Place,
Hatfield, Hertfordshire AL9 6JE, United Kingdom.

Telephone: +44 (0)1707 642629
Fax: +44 (0)1707 663041

# THE LATE DAME BARBARA CARTLAND

Barbara Cartland who sadly died in May 2000 at the age of nearly 99 was the world's most famous romantic novelist who wrote 723 books in her lifetime with worldwide sales of over 1 billion copies and her books were translated into 36 different languages.

As well as romantic novels, she wrote historical biographies, 6 autobiographies, theatrical plays, books of advice on life, love, vitamins and cookery. She also found time to be a political speaker and television and radio personality.

She wrote her first book at the age of 21 and this was called *Jigsaw*. It became an immediate bestseller and sold 100,000 copies in hardback and was translated into 6 different languages. She wrote continuously throughout her life, writing bestsellers for an astonishing 76 years. Her books have always been immensely popular in the United States, where in 1976 her current books were at numbers 1 & 2 in the B. Dalton bestsellers list, a feat never achieved before or since by any author.

Barbara Cartland became a legend in her own lifetime and will be best remembered for her wonderful romantic novels, so loved by her millions of readers throughout the world.

Her books will always be treasured for their moral message, her pure and innocent heroines, her good looking and dashing heroes and above all her belief that the power of love is more important than anything else in everyone's life.

*"When the world becomes more and more troubled, everyone should look to God for guidance and to love for happiness. There is no other way."*

Barbara Cartland

# CHAPTER ONE
# 1833

"You will do just as I tell you. This man is a good match and you should thank Heaven on your knees for him."

"Well, I don't. I will not marry a man I have never met. If he is anything like his father, he will be repulsive. I will not marry him and that's final."

"Just don't you speak to me like that, my girl. I am your father and you owe me respect, so don't forget it."

"You are *not* my father, you're my stepfather. Papa was a good kind man, who would never have tried to force me into marriage with a man merely because he was rich."

In the drawing room of Gardner Manor a man and a young girl faced each other, both furiously angry.

John Gardner was in his fifties – blunt, red-faced, brutal. His stepdaughter, the Lady Selina Napier, was just nineteen, elegant, slender and fragile in build, but strong in spirit.

She faced this menacing man with her head high.

She disliked him intensely, had always disliked him ever since the day he had married her mother, the widowed Countess Napier. It seemed to her that he brought an evil spirit into the house.

Selina's parents had been blissfully happy.

Her father, the Earl, would have so liked a son and they would both have loved a little more money.

1

They had so little that they were forced to abandon his ancestral home and live in a modest house on the estate. But none of this could really spoil their happiness because they loved each other so deeply.

Selina had been only fifteen when disaster struck.

Her father had fallen out hunting and his horse had rolled on him, crushing him.

He sadly had lived only a week.

The tragedy had shattered her mother. For a year she was miserable. Sometimes she would wander through the house, looking distracted, as if by a miracle she would find the man she loved.

And then after a year, she had suddenly announced that she intended to marry again.

Her choice was John Gardner, a shipbuilder with a large amount of money. He gave her many expensive gifts and to Selina too, which the child received with a forced hostile politeness.

She distrusted him from the first moment.

The marriage took place quickly and secretly, as if her mother was too ashamed for her friends and family to know about it.

As well she might be, Selina thought.

Before she married Lord Napier she had been Lady Edwina Franklin. Now she became Lady Edwina Gardner, something that nobody could overlook as her new husband always introduced her by that title and never referred to her as anything but 'Lady Edwina'.

And he always referred to his stepdaughter as 'Lady Selina Napier'. Lacking a title himself, he allowed no one to forget that he had acquired two titled ladies by marriage.

'He is a snob,' she told herself. 'He married Mama just to advance himself socially. He has no breeding, only money. He throws it around, trying to impress the world and only makes people despise him.'

He had taken them out of their little house and into the vast grandiose mansion he had purchased and renamed 'Gardner Manor', to the amusement, Selina was convinced, of all his well-born neighbours.

It was far too large for the three of them and needed an army of staff for the sixty rooms and extensive gardens. But it lived up to what John Gardner felt was his dignity.

"A fit setting for a Countess," he had often carolled, ignoring the fact that his wife was no longer a Countess.

He surrounded them with every luxury that Selina realised her mother really enjoyed.

For a nice comfortable life she was well prepared to put up with her husband's vulgar ways.

She entertained his business friends, assuming the lofty manner that he liked to see.

Whenever she could she would persuade some of her aristocratic friends to visit, but this was rare. Many were reluctant because his behaviour embarrassed them.

And then without any warning Lady Edwina caught influenza in the middle of winter and died.

True to form John Gardner gave her a lavish funeral and built a big extravagant monument on which the words 'Lady Edwina Gardner' were carved in large letters.

He paraded his grief to the world and if Selina could have believed it genuine, she might have warmed to him.

But very soon it became apparent that he planned to dragoon her into providing him with a ladder into Society.

He refused to allow her to go and live with friends of her father. At most he would allow her to pay them odd visits and he would insist on accompanying her. Gradually the invitations dried up.

As time passed Selina found that she was squirming when he rolled out her title in introducing her to strangers as if he was sharing something very valuable with them.

He embarrassed her by the way he boasted about his late wife and told strangers how heart-broken he had been by the death of 'Lady Edwina'.

But the strangers who came into the house now her mother was no longer there were mostly men with whom her stepfather was doing a deal or those he believed could help him in his social climbing.

"Why won't you allow me to leave?" she asked him again and again.

"I want you with me."

"Why do you want me? After all I can hardly help you build a ship."

Her stepfather had laughed and it was not a pleasant sound.

"You can do so much more than that," he said. "The people I bring here like to meet you. You're an attraction to them. Surely it's not too much to ask in return for all I have given you?"

"I never asked you to give me all those expensive gifts," she cried. "They were not really for me, anyway, or for my mother. You just wanted to deck us out to impress the world.

"Neither Mama nor I cared for it. My father never had any money, but she was far happier with him than she ever was with you, because they truly loved each other!"

"Nonsense! Everyone I know appreciates money and that includes you, my girl. That wonderful father of yours couldn't leave you a single penny. You depend on me for every stitch you're wearing, so don't you forget it!"

It was true.

She was trapped.

And then one fine day he returned from Portsmouth, where he had been to inspect one of his ships and there was something about him that troubled her more than ever.

She was used to his unpleasant tempers but his good humours disturbed her more.

"I have some excellent news," he announced.

Selina tried to look interested.

"I know that it will please you as much as it pleases me," he declared.

She doubted it. It was more than likely to be his way of telling her that she had better be pleased or there would be trouble.

She knew that her worst fears were realised when he added,

"*I have found you a husband*."

Selina stared at him.

"What are you saying?"

"He's just the son of one of the richest men in the country. You haven't met him, but you will. When his father approached me, I realised at once that this was the ideal match for you."

"I don't know what you can be talking about. Why should I marry someone I have never met?"

She spoke almost aggressively, but at the same time she felt rather unnerved. There was something in his voice and the way he was looking at her was unusual.

It was something she had not noticed in him before.

"Now sit down and listen to what I have to say," he ordered, "You are the right age, you are also extremely attractive and you're the daughter of an Earl – you have a title."

"To be Lady Selina is hardly an important title."

"It will just have to do," he said flatly. "With your connections and Peter Turner's money the world is going to be made very aware of you, my dear child."

The last words were added awkwardly as though he was remembering lines in a script. He was playing the role of the loving father, but he had not quite got the hang of it.

"Peter Turner?" she queried. "Can he be the son of Ralph Turner that dreadful man who was here two months ago and breathed whisky fumes all over me?"

"Whatever do you mean – dreadful?" he snapped. "Ralph Turner has fifty thousand pounds a year."

She was now beginning to grow angry as well as apprehensive.

"If he had a million pounds a year he would still be dreadful," she asserted flatly.

John Gardner gasped. For once in his life he was completely taken aback. He had never heard of such an idea before.

How could you possibly be dreadful if you had so much money? It was practically blasphemy.

"If he's so very rich, why is he bothering with me?" Selina demanded. "Why not the daughter of a Duke or a Marquis, preferably one who's alive and can introduce him into the right circles?"

Her stepfather grew testy.

"Never mind that."

"We do know the answer, don't we?" she persisted. "Turner is such an appalling man that no money on earth could buy his son into those circles. So he'll settle for *me*."

"And you should be glad of it," he bawled. "Where else are you going to find a husband? You haven't a penny of your own."

"Then I'll manage without. Money or no money, I will not marry a man I do not love and who does not love me for myself."

"Peter will love you," he replied impatiently, "you need not worry about that. His father will not only make you one of the richest couples in England, but as he told me himself, when he dies, every penny he possesses – and I can assure you that it is enormous – will be inherited by Peter."

He paused and as Selina did not speak he went on,

"You can shine in Society. Everyone will want to come to your parties, even Royalty."

There was silence whilst Selina started at him. At last she responded,

"Do you really believe that kind of life, exciting though it sounds, would be worth marrying a man I do not know, who can scarcely want to marry me when he has never even met me?"

"He has heard all about you," her stepfather replied. "His father not only told him how important you are, but also that you are so beautiful. I gave him a painting, which was in your mother's bedroom for him to see that we were not exaggerating your beauty.

"Although it was painted over three years ago, you are fifty times better looking today than you were then."

Selina rose and walked to the window standing with her back to her stepfather. She knew by the lilt in his voice that this arrangement meant a great deal to him.

He was very obviously determined that she should do what he wanted.

From the very moment he had married her mother he had always expected that anything he demanded should be his.

He had discussed this with Peter Turner's father and together they would insist on having their own way. No

7

amount of protestations would ever be listened to or even considered.

She remembered the day he had left for Portsmouth, he had seemed agitated. For once his mind had not been solely on business, which usually concerned him more than anything else. There had been something new and curious in the way he looked at her and spoke to her.

But she could not have possibly imagined then the monstrous idea that he had just put before her.

She turned round to face him, ready for battle. But for the moment it seemed that he would try another tack.

"Now come along. Let's have no more foolishness. I want you to tell me that you are a little grateful to me and looking forward to the exciting life I've provided for you."

"I cannot agree," she now told him. "I want to be married when I am in love. Money alone is not enough to make any woman happy."

"Nonsense! Nonsense! All women require money! You like pretty dresses, don't you?"

"I hardly think that any dresses are enough to make a happy marriage," Selina replied. "I have no intention of marrying anyone unless I love him as much as Mama loved my Papa."

She spoke out bravely even though she felt a little quiver go through her as her stepfather's eyes darkened and he stared at her with a furious expression that made her shiver.

"You'll damned well do as you are told!" he said sharply. His voice rose almost to a scream. "You will be rich! *Rich*! Horses, carriages, a house in London, parties."

Seeing no hint of any interest in her face he grew angrier, the words almost tumbling over themselves.

"What more could you ever desire? God knows

most women would now go down on their knees and thank Heaven itself for such an opportunity."

Then Selina countered,

"It is just not enough. I want love. The love which cannot be bought with money."

"That is the sort of damned silly thing you would say," her stepfather shouted. "You will do as you are told! Peter is coming here tomorrow to propose to you and you will accept him!

"If you try to disobey me, I will beat you all the way to the Church."

With that he walked out of the room, slamming the door behind him.

Selina put her hand up to her forehead.

Then, as she felt suddenly weak with the horror of it all, she collapsed onto a sofa.

She was trembling.

Her stepfather had now finally revealed himself as he really was.

Next she jumped up and hurried out of the room.

Then she started to run as fast as she could down the passage, out through the door and into the garden.

Only when she reached the thickness of the orchard did she stop running. She sat down on a fallen tree and put her hands up to her face.

The sun was shining and the birds were singing, but all she could think of was the terrible scene she had just endured and the ugliness of John Gardner's mind.

'Whatever can I do?' she asked herself. 'How can I avoid it?'

But when she asked herself the question again, she knew there was only one answer.

She must run away and hide.

Selina had always been instructed by her father and mother to think things over and never to act impulsively.

So she began by going to her room, sitting down, and thinking hard about what she meant to do.

But however hard she thought about it, she always came back to the same answer. There was only one way to avoid the horror planned for her and that was to disappear.

And she must act quickly.

If Peter Turner was coming tomorrow then she must leave tonight.

She heard a noise from below and looked out to see her stepfather departing in a chaise.

To her relief she recalled that he was attending a meeting this evening with the Lord Lieutenant concerning various charities. He was always generous to charities as a way of elevating his own importance, so he would be away for hours.

Now was her chance.

Hurriedly she began to pack some things together.

Then she went into her mother's room. Because she did not know how long she would be away, she would take some memento of Mama. Not her expensive jewels which had been given to her by John Gardner, but her wedding ring, which dear Papa had put on her hand.

Back in her own room she looked through her jewel box and discarded the fine gifts her stepfather had given to her. She wanted as little of his as possible.

He had sometimes given her money, not so much in a kindly way but like a man tossing a bone to a dog.

Selina had passed on much of the money to charity, but his last present lay where she had left it. She took it, now promising herself that one day she would give it back.

From the jewel box she took only a silver necklace that had been her mother's when Papa was alive.

There were now quite a lot of packed cases and she wondered how she could possibly get them away without attracting too much attention.

She went to the stables and found the old groom.

"What can I do for you, Miss Selina?" he enquired, smiling. "Surely you don't want to go riding at this hour?"

"No, I want to take the dog cart," she said. "I am visiting a friend and taking some clothes to be sold at the charity bazaar in a week or so."

"Very well, miss. Do you want me to drive you?"

"Thank you, but I would prefer to drive myself. It's not far."

She hurried back upstairs and dressed herself in her travelling gown.

She summoned one of her stepfather's footmen to take her bags and then she found the dog cart ready with her cases in the back.

The groom made one more attempt to persuade her to let him drive, but she smiled and refused firmly. Then she made her escape while she still could.

She moved swiftly along the road and there seemed to be very little traffic about.

'I love the country,' thought Selina. 'But if I hide in London, it may be much more difficult for him to find me. And that is all that matters. So, it must be London.'

As soon as possible she turned off the beaten track, avoiding the villages where she would be known.

When the hue and cry began, the fewer people who had seen her, the better.

After two long hours she was thinking that sooner or later she must begin to look for a place to stay the night.

She drove down quite a narrow lane on which there were practically no cottages, when she was suddenly aware that there were three men on horseback just ahead of her.

She slowed the dog cart down and was wondering who they were and if by chance they would recognise her, when she realised that they were wearing masks.

With a feeling of shock and fear, she recognised that they were highwaymen. If only she could turn round and go back! But the lane was too narrow.

Now it was too late to do anything. She could only pull in her horse as two of them blocked the road in front of her.

One of the men spoke first and ordered the others,

"Open this 'ere gate and take the lady with 'er dog cart into the field!"

"What – do you want?" Selina asked nervously.

She realised they were all set on robbing her. They would take her money and maybe her luggage, leaving her with nothing and no means of making her escape.

As they entered the field, the one who had given the orders came alongside and demanded,

"All right, where's the money. Hand it over."

"I am afraid – I have practically nothing – because I am merely going out to dinner – with some friends."

The man looked into the dog cart and remarked,

"With three cases! If you ask me you're goin' away for an 'oliday and 'olidays are expensive."

"Oh, please, please don't stop me," begged Selina. "I'm really very hard up."

"So are we," the highwayman replied with a laugh. "And our problems are more important to us than yours."

But even as he spoke there was the sound of a gun being fired, which resounded through the trees.

As the highwaymen all turned round to look, a man riding a horse and carrying a gun came towards them.

"Now, I told you boys," he called out, as he drew up beside them, "that I would not have you robbing people on my land."

"We didn't mean to be on your land, my Lord," the chief highwayman replied. "But the gate was open and, as you know, us don't want to be seen on the road."

"Be off with all of you," the stranger ordered them sternly.

The highwayman suddenly did not seem so fierce as he hesitated for a moment. Then he said hopefully,

"We'll all pretty hungry, my Lord."

"All right then. Here's money. Go get yourselves something to eat and stay off my land."

"Thank you, thank you very much, my Lord."

Then without saying anything further all three of the highwaymen trotted away and Selina was left staring.

"Thank you," she said. "I was so scared they would rob me of everything. But didn't you want to turn them over to the law?"

The man laughed.

"It would only make a bad situation worse. They are just young boys and basically harmless. They don't carry weapons. If they did, I *would* turn them over to the law. But they are bored and cannot obtain any work, so they become 'highwaymen'. It's mostly a game to them.

"They are not very good at it and I usually end up paying for their supper."

"I think it is very kind of you and I am very grateful you came when you did."

"If you ask me it is a mistake for you to be driving about late at night and the sooner you go home the better."

As she regarded him she now realised that he was exceedingly good-looking and obviously a gentleman.

Just the same she thought it strange he should be so kind to the highwaymen.

"The real fact is, I am running away," she confided. "Can you tell me where there is a respectable inn where I might stay the night?"

"Running away!" he exclaimed. "Why should you be doing that?"

Selina hesitated and then she responded,

"Because I have to. I just can't tell you any more. Please don't press me."

"But you really cannot travel alone like this, all by yourself!"

"I didn't dare ask anyone to come with me in case they betrayed me."

"You're a positive invitation to robbers and the next time it may not be a schoolboy prank. It's getting late and I don't really know of a respectable inn, except one several miles away."

"Can you direct me please?"

"I have no intention of doing so. I don't want you on my conscience. I think that I should take you home and keep you safe until tomorrow."

"Thank you, but I really don't think I can go home with you," Selina asserted quickly.

"You're perfectly right to be careful," said the man. "But my housekeeper, who is a dear old woman, will act as your chaperone."

"Where do you live?" she asked cautiously.

Although he had the manners and air of a gentleman what she could make out of his clothes in the fast fading light seemed rough, even a little shabby.

"At Castleton Hall," he replied. "It's only a couple of miles from here."

"Castleton – ?" she wrinkled her pretty brow, trying to recall the name.

"The home of the Marquis of Castleton."

"But won't he mind you taking me to his home?"

"I promise you that nobody shall trouble you?"

"Well, I expect it's a very big place and you could hide me away so that he would never know."

"It is certainly a very big place," he agreed gravely. "Too big for one man. Let us be on our way."

"You are very kind. Are you quite certain I am not being an encumbrance?"

"Not at all. I was not looking forward to talking to myself at dinner and it will be more interesting to hear your story."

Selina laughed.

"That will take a little time."

"Then I shall look forward to it. Follow me."

He turned his horse round and Selina followed him.

'This is surely such an adventure,' she told herself, 'and one I never expected in my wildest dream.'

# CHAPTER TWO

They passed over several fields. Then through the trees she could see a magnificent house.

It was obviously ancient and seemed most attractive with tall trees towering behind it and the garden filled with brilliant flowers.

As they drew nearer Selina could see there was a stream at the bottom of the garden that ended behind a small wood.

Her rescuer crossed the stream over an old bridge, then he turned right towards the back of the house. Selina following him, realised they were making for the stables.

She was safe and in her heart she felt it must be due to her mother and father who had led her into safety at least for tonight whatever tomorrow might bring.

The moment they entered the stables, two grooms ran to her dog cart and as she climbed out, another servant appeared who was obviously a footman, as he was wearing livery.

He began to take down her cases and walked away with them in the direction of the house.

Her host indicated for her to follow him, but they did not, as she expected, go to the rear of the great house. Instead he headed towards the front door.

"Will it be all right to go in there?" she asked, not wanting him to get into trouble.

He gave her a kindly smile and she thought what a pleasant face he had.

"I think so," he answered.

Selina thought that the house was one of the most delightful and impressive places she had ever seen.

She had visited a number of great houses when her mother had been alive, yet this great house was even more beautiful than any house she had ever seen before.

There were flowers growing round the front and a clematis fully in bloom was climbing up over the door.

The moment they appeared the door opened.

When Selina walked in, she saw there was not only a butler waiting for them but four footmen wearing a very smart livery.

There was no sign of her luggage and she imagined the men who had taken it from the stables had handed it in at the back door and it would be waiting for her upstairs.

Almost as if she had said it aloud, her rescuer now suggested,

"I expect, as you have been driving for quite some time, you would like to wash and change before dinner."

"That sounds delightful," she replied. "I have been driving for too long."

"There is no hurry," he told her, "and Newton, the butler, will show you to your room."

Selina smiled at him,

"Thank you very much."

"Don't hurry. I am certain that you will enjoy your dinner here much more than where you were thinking of dining."

"You do know the answer to that question and once again let me say I am very grateful to you."

She followed the butler up the stairs and when they reached the first floor, he pointed to a large door.

She saw as she entered that the windows looked out over the garden and as she gazed around she gasped aloud.

The room was simply staggering. There was a vast four-poster bed with golden hangings of silk brocade.

Two young maids came in and gave bob curtseys before starting to unpack her bags and hang up her clothes.

Then they carried in a large jug of water with which she could wash and helped her to undress.

The warm water seemed to wash away not only the dust that had fallen on her when she was driving, but some of the anxiety as to what would happen when her stepfather found she had disappeared.

'At least,' she mused, 'he would not, in his wildest imagination, think of me being so comfortable here!'

She laughed to herself.

'It seems quite extraordinary that I am now staying in this house with a man whose name I don't know!'

She almost asked the maids to tell her who was the owner of the house.

Then she thought they would think it very strange to be staying without being aware of who her host was.

'I expect he'll tell me when I come downstairs for dinner,' she told herself. 'I wonder if I should tell him who I really am or whether it would be wiser to be anonymous.'

She was still worrying over this question when she dressed herself in one of her prettiest evening gowns.

She never imagined she would be wearing it under such odd circumstances, but she was determined to enjoy her adventure to the full.

After all when there would be another one?

There was a knock on her door and it was a maid.

"If you will please follow me, miss."

She led Selina down the huge stairway, which was of a very attractive pale grey stone and into the front hall. Now she had more time to look about her she saw that the hall had a military nature. Many weapons were arranged in patterns on the walls and suits of armour stood in corners.

There was a baffling myriad of corridors, too many to remember and then the maid opened up a pair of double doors and ushered Selina into the drawing room.

For a moment she stood in awe and gazed at all the luxury and beauty. The gilt decorated ceiling was divided into semicircular compartments, each of which contained a painting of some mythical scene.

The gilt motif was continued on the walls that were covered in cream and gold panels interspersed with large mirrors.

There were two huge fireplaces of Italian marble, and beside one stood a gentleman elegantly dressed in his evening clothes.

His snowy shirt was ruffled and embroidered and at his throat flashed a diamond tiepin.

"I am sorry," said Selina quickly. "I thought – oh, goodness! It's *you*!"

"A very good evening," he began, smiling at her. "Yes, indeed it's me. Allow me to introduce myself. The Marquis of Castleton at your service, ma'am."

"Oh, how silly of me not to have realised," Selina exclaimed. "It's just that – "

"Just that I looked like one of my own workmen! It was wrong of me to tease you. I do apologise."

"There is no need," she smiled.

"Do you like my house?"

"Yes, it is so beautiful. I know I have read about it somewhere as one of the very oldest and most magnificent houses in England and please do promise me that before I leave I may see much more of it than I have seen already."

"You will see exactly what you want," the Marquis promised. "At the same time, you know my name, but I'm still waiting to hear who you are!"

She hesitated.

"Trust me," added the Marquis, reading her face.

"I promised myself when I ran away – that I would never tell anyone who I am – just in case they told – *him* where I was. He would find me and take me back."

She spoke very hesitatingly and the Marquis paused before he assured her,

"I swear on the Bible, if necessary, that I will never tell anyone who you are. I also promise I will try to protect you from anything dangerous or unpleasant."

Selina gave a deep sigh.

"Thank you, thank you," she whispered. "I've been so frightened – and I've been praying all the way here that no one would find out that I had run away until I was really safe."

"You are safe here for the time being. I will keep your identity a secret for as long as you want me to."

"And you won't make me go back?

"My word on it. Please tell me who you are."

"My father was Lord Napier, but he and my mother are both dead."

"I have heard of your father's name from my own father. I think they were at school together."

"My father was at Eton and Oxford."

"Then I was right. That was where my father went. He often talked of the friends he knew at school. I knew I had heard the name before.

"I am proud and delighted to entertain his daughter, and even more glad to think that I saved her, tonight at any rate, from some uncomfortable village inn!"

"I've been thinking that ever since I arrived here," Selina replied. "In fact, my Lord – "

"Please," he interrupted her, "my name is Ian."

"And I am Selina."

"Selina suits you," the Marquis told her gravely. "It is original and unusual, both of which you are."

"I am only glad that you are not shocked, as many would be, because I am running away and hiding from my stepfather."

"No, I am not shocked. I am certain that you had a good reason for what you felt you had to do. Now, let us enjoy a glass of champagne before dinner and drink each other's health. Having saved you from one disaster, I hope I am able to do so again in the future!"

"Thank you very much," she said fervently. "I was so terrified when I saw those highwaymen, because if they had robbed me, I would have had to return back home and I would rather die."

The Marquis put a glass of champagne in her hand.

"Don't think about it. What we have to decide now is what you will do in the future. You must not take such risks again as you took today. I am horrified at the thought of you alone with no one to protect you from danger."

The door opened and the butler announced,

"Dinner is served, my Lord."

Selina drank a little of the champagne and then the Marquis held out his hand.

"Come along now, we both deserve a good dinner. When we have eaten, the future will seem brighter."

"I hope you are right," replied Selina.

She took his arm and they walked through the door and down the passage to the dining room.

This was even more impressive than the drawing room. There was a long polished table and the candlesticks surrounding a bowl of fruit were exquisite and were echoed by those on the mantelpiece and side tables.

There were pictures on the walls which she knew had been painted by a famous French artist.

The Marquis seated himself at the top of the table and she sat on his right.

The food was delicious and so was the wine.

They were served in great state by the butler with the assistance of two footmen in livery and powdered wigs. Once a course had been served the butler left the room, but the footmen went to stand by the walls.

As though conscious of their presence, the Marquis lowered his voice to talk of a visit he had recently made to Europe.

He described, to Selina's great delight, some of the pictures he had seen in the Louvre and the horses he had admired in the Bois de Boulogne at the races.

"How I envy you your travels."

"You have never travelled?"

"When Papa was alive we were too poor. But once my stepfather took my mother and me across to Le Havre for a few days. He is a shipbuilder, so Le Havre was of great interest to him. Mama and I would have liked to see Paris, but after a few days in Le Havre we came home."

She glanced over her shoulder at the footmen.

"Yes, I can find them oppressive sometimes," the Marquis remarked with his quiet kind smile.

She considered that everything about him was quiet and kind. He smiled but he did not laugh and gravity was evidently natural to him.

She tried to guess at his age, but could only decide that he was in his late thirties.

'Almost old enough to be my father,' she pondered from the standpoint of nineteen. 'Well – an uncle.'

At any rate it made it acceptable for her to be here alone with him.

His face was handsome and might have been very striking if it had been livelier. But an air of melancholy seemed rather natural to him. Even his smiles had a touch of gravity.

"If you find them oppressive, why don't you send them away?" she enquired. "You are the Master."

"Am I? At times I feel more like a slave – a slave to this house and its traditions, a slave to my title and all that it entails, and a slave to the generations of my family, who sometimes still seem to be present, silently telling me what they require of me.

"Those footmen stood like that in my father's day, and my grandfather's day!"

Selina lowered her voice and added dramatically,

"They're probably the very same footmen!"

He gave a faint choke of laughter and regarded her with appreciation.

"What a thought, but I don't think they can be! I'll swear they actually move from time to time. A little more wine?"

"Thank you, just a very little."

He reached for the decanter, but instantly a footman glided forward to perform the service for him.

"You see?" he said, when the footman had retreated to the wall. "I am not allowed to do anything."

He checked himself suddenly.

"Listen, Selina, it's unforgivable of me to make fun of them. They are all good fellows and I know each one of them individually.

"I even know the names of all their children, which rather shocks the old guard, I am afraid. I am supposed to rise loftily above such knowledge, but I cannot do it."

"Good for you," Selina came in at once. "I believe it's nice to be friends with your servants."

"*Friends*?" he echoed with mock horror. "What are you thinking of? The Heavens would fall!"

"But you could assert yourself," suggested Selina.

He thought about her remark for a moment.

"I'm not really a very assertive person," he said at last, almost apologetically. "In an emergency I daresay I could be as decisive as any other man. But in this house, weighed down by all its traditions – well, I know my place, and it isn't a comfortable place.

"The merest kitchen maid can turn me to jelly by saying, 'that is how it was done in the old days, my Lord.' They add in the 'my Lord' just to give me the illusion of authority. And I say, 'Oh, was it?' And creep away!"

"Now you're making fun of me," protested Selina.

"No, of myself. Perhaps I am exaggerating, but not by much."

"But you are *the Marquis*."

"And Marquises are meant to be assertive, I know. But you see, I wasn't meant to be the Marquis. I had an older brother, Jack, who would have been ideal. He was a big strong strapping fellow.

"I was rather puny when I was born and they didn't expect me to survive long, which was useful because I was allowed to go my own way. Jack was the roisterer, I was the scholar. He and I were very close, although we were so different.

"He took my side when I said I wanted to go into the Church. Our father was horrified. He thought I would end up as a curate in a remote country parish, which was exactly what would have suited me best. But when I tried to explain this to Papa, Jack muttered, 'shut up and leave this to me'."

"What did he do?" Selina asked, much entertained.

"He told my father grandiose tales about how the family influence could raise me in the Church. According to him I would be Archbishop of Canterbury in no time.

"I did have qualms of conscience about feeding him such fairy tales, but Jack grabbed me and hissed, 'do you really want to be ordained or don't you?' And I did, so I swallowed my conscience, thanked my father before he could change his mind and entered Theological College."

A look of inexpressible sadness came over his face.

"What happened?" asked Selina.

"In the middle of my first term I was summoned to go home because Jack was dying. Galloping consumption. He had been coughing for some time but ignored it. When he went to a doctor it was too late. It swept through him. I arrived in time to spend an hour with him."

"Oh no," she whispered. "And he was your dearest friend, wasn't he?"

"Yes he was. My very dearest and only true friend. I have never been as close to another human being as I was to Jack and I never expect to be.

"On his death bed he said, 'sorry, old boy. It's all going to fall on to you now. Dreadful thing to do to you.'

Then the family came in and we all said goodbye. His very last word was for me. He gave my hand a faint squeeze, and murmured, '*sorry*,' again. Then he died."

He was silent a long time after that story.

Hardly knowing what she was doing Selina reached out her hand and touched his. He reacted at once, closing his fingers over it and holding tightly.

"His death was the end of everything. It killed my parents. They both followed him in a year, and here was I, on my own, in this great echoing mausoleum, cut off from the life I love, doing a job I am not equipped for."

Suddenly he seemed to notice their clasped hands and disengaged himself quickly, saying to the butler who had appeared again,

"By the way, Newton, send someone to ensure that the gate into the orchard is locked. Those silly boys who think they are highwaymen opened it again today."

"Your servants must think it very strange you being friends with the highwaymen," Selina remarked when the butler had bowed and left.

"They are used to me being friends with all sorts of strange people," replied the Marquis. "They disapprove but they put it down to 'Lordly eccentricity'.

"Actually the highwaymen are somewhat special as their parents were employed on the estate. Although they are behaving badly, I feel I have to look after them and if nothing else prevent them from going to prison."

"That's very kind of you, but I always thought that highwaymen were very dangerous. I read some time ago that two of them were shot and killed while trying to hold up a mail carriage."

"I remember that story. Apparently they were shot as soon as they appeared which I think is shocking. They should have been threatened first, so that they could realise the danger and have second thoughts."

Selina nodded.

"I hate to think of a man being killed unnecessarily. That's why wars are so frightening. To all of us, whether we are rich or poor, life is precious."

The Marquis smiled at her.

"That is something I have often thought myself, but I didn't expect to hear a woman say it."

"I think that women are more afraid of battles and people being killed than men. They're denied the relief of action and remain at home to pray for their loved ones."

"Yes, I think you are right," he concurred, speaking with his usual gravity.

When at last they were alone in the drawing room and were seated on a sofa, the Marquis asked her,

"Now we are alone and no one is listening, tell me about yourself and what was so dreadful that a young lady like you felt that she had to take such terrible risks."

"Because there was nothing else I could do."

"Are you quite sure?"

"Absolutely sure," replied Selina. "And as I don't want you to feel burdened with my difficulties, it might be best for me to say nothing."

"Best for whom? Certainly not best for you. I will help you in every way possible, but I simply cannot allow you to leave here and go out alone into a world of which you know nothing. In fact, if you don't tell me everything, I shall not permit you to leave!"

"Not permit me?" she demanded, indignantly. "Am I your prisoner then?"

"If necessary. I don't want to have your fate on my conscience."

"What I do is entirely my decision!"

"Not entirely. I know far more of the world than you and I'll keep you here by any means necessary until I am assured of your safety."

"Then you are worse than my stepfather. He would have imprisoned me if I had not run away first."

"I am beginning to have some sympathy with him!"

"How can you say that? He is a wicked, monstrous man."

Selina felt so upset that she jumped up and began to stride about the room, almost in tears. At once the Marquis rose and followed her, full of contrition.

"Selina, please forgive me. I had no right to speak to you like that. Listen to me, please – "

He managed to make her stop and held her hands.

"It is unforgivable of me to upset you, when you've been so much upset already. But after all – " he gave her a wry self-mocking smile, "it was you who had said I should assert myself."

"I didn't mean against me," she moaned.

"I know. I did warn you that I did it badly. Please don't cry."

"I'm not crying," she asserted fiercely. "What do you think I am, a crybaby?"

"No, I think you are a very brave young woman and I only want to help you. If you would only – "

He broke off sharply as the door opened and the butler entered.

"Excuse me, my Lord, this letter's been delivered at the front door with instructions that I was to give it to your Lordship immediately."

As he spoke he held out a silver salver on which lay a letter. The Marquis took it and examined it, frowning.

"How did this get here?" he asked.

"A groom brought it on horseback, my Lord."

"Tell him to take his horse to the stables and give him a bed for the night."

"Very good, my Lord."

The butler closed the door and the Marquis, holding the letter walked to the window. Selina saw him open the envelope.

He read the letter and then read it again. Selina, watching, thought that the contents disturbed him. At last he came back and sat down beside her.

She thought he looked rather grave, but did not like to ask him any questions.

"Now we will continue," he said. "You must listen to me. You really cannot go on alone. You may be lucky, but you may not. It will not only be highwaymen you have to battle against, but men. Men who will be struck by your beauty. Men who will perhaps frighten you and there will be no one to turn to for help."

"Then I must now tell you why I have run away and perhaps then you will understand. I told you that I would rather die than go back *and I mean it*."

"You must not say such things. After all you are very beautiful, very young and the world is at your feet."

"I do so wish it was true," replied Selina. "But you cannot imagine my world."

"We have delayed long enough," said the Marquis firmly. "Now the time has come when you must tell me everything."

# CHAPTER THREE

There was a short silence.

Then slowly almost as if he was compelling her to do so, Selina told him first how her father had died, then her mother, lonely miserable and in poor health, had married again as she was too unhappy to face life alone.

"I was too young at the time to be of any help to her. She was alone and miserable and I think she turned to my stepfather simply because she needed comfort."

"I can easily understand. Do go on."

"She married a certain John Gardner, who is very rich. My mother's father was Lord Franklin and he felt that marriage to an Earl's daughter would provide him with a place in Society that all his money could not to buy him.

"He wanted to be socially equal to landowners, who were not impressed by his money. He always felt like an outsider and it made him bitter.

"He tried hard to present himself as a great landed gentleman. His shipbuilding business is in Portsmouth, so you would think he would want to live there.

"But great landowners do not live close to trade, so he bought this enormous estate in Hampshire, because he thought it would give him the right background. It takes him three days to drive to Portsmouth."

"Which is foolish of him," the Marquis observed. "But there is no end to the vanities of snobbery. Now, tell me, where do you come into all this?"

"He is determined to use me to further his Social ambitions. If only you could witness him introduce me as *Lady* Selina, as he used to introduce my mother as *Lady* Edwina.

"I could have easily put up with him if he had been a genuinely kind man, but all he thinks about is money and what it can buy him.

"He sent me to Finishing School in France because he felt it would make me more aristocratic and 'polished', but he brought me back after only one term. I think he was afraid for me to be out sight for too long in case I escaped.

"He has a friend who is also in business and as rich as he is. The friend has a son whom he wants to move into Society, which apparently at the moment is taking little, if any, notice of him."

"How does he mean to do so?" the Marquis asked.

"By marrying me," Selina replied in a low voice.

"Marrying you!"

"He desires to 'acquire' me, because I am a *lady*," she explained ironically. "And my stepfather is determined that I shall agree."

"But why? If Gardner has these social ambitions and money, why doesn't he try to marry you to a title?"

"I too wondered about that. I think he knows it's impossible. He is such a dreadful man that nobody with a title would marry me if it meant taking him into the family for all his money. So this is the next best thing.

"There's always been a kind of rivalry between him and Ralph Turner as to who can make the most money and who can do the best deals. Turner is a lot richer, but my stepfather is ahead of him at the moment, because of me."

"Because you are *Lady* Selina?"

"That's right. To him I am a bargaining chip. He will use me to unite the two fortunes and Peter Turner and

I will live so lavishly that Society will *have* to accept us. That's what he thinks will happen."

"What's he like, this man he wants you to marry?"

"I've never met him, but I've met his father. He is a horrible little man who drinks from dawn until dusk and breathes whiskey fumes over the whole world."

"Meaning you?"

"Yes," she admitted with a shudder.

There was silence for a moment. Then the Marquis exploded,

"I've never heard anything so disgraceful."

"How can I marry a man I have never seen and let him touch me?"

"Of course you must not do so! I can understand why you ran away. In fact, there was nothing else that you could do. We have to think of a solution to this problem."

"Do you really mean it? Please, *please* help me. I have no one else to turn to."

"But surely your mother had friends you could stay with or perhaps relations who would take you in?"

"I wanted to go to them when Mama died, but *he* wouldn't let me. I could hardly go to them now, because they just don't know me. Papa and Mama were so happy together they did not worry about their relations. I doubt if they'd really be pleased if I turned up on their doorstep."

"As I have said, I can fully appreciate why you've run away. But are you quite sure that your stepfather will force you to marry this man?"

"I am quite certain from what he has already said that he will force me up the aisle, whatever my objections."

There was a fear in her voice that told the Marquis her feelings were very real and she was not exaggerating.

He rose from the sofa and walked to the window. She saw him draw from his pocket the letter that had just arrived.

He read it through again before putting it back into the envelope.

He seemed sunk in thought and Selina wondered if he was regretting that he had promised to help her.

After all, why should her troubles be of any interest to him, when he clearly had troubles of his own?

She pressed her lips together just in case she should plead with him for help again. She simply must not do so.

Then, as if the Marquis had made up his mind, he turned from the window, walked to the sofa and sat down.

Taking Selina's hand in his he began,

"I have an interesting proposition to make to you. An idea which, if you agree, would help us both."

She looked at him in surprise.

"Of course, I shall be glad to help you in any way I can after all your kindness to me."

"Thank you so much, Selina. The fact is that I have a problem which is as difficult for me as yours is for you."

Selina thought this was unlikely. It seemed to her that men always found it easier to escape their dilemmas than women, but she responded,

"Tell me how I can help you."

He hesitated, as though he could not think how to begin.

"Recently," he answered at last, "I was staying with a family I've known for years, who have always been very kind and helpful to me."

He stopped.

Selina wondered why this story should upset him, as it obviously did.

"On this occasion there was a large house party and we had dancing after dinner every night. One girl, called Felicity, was a particularly good dancer and I competed with two other men to secure her as my partner – "

He smiled as he continued,

"I was more successful than they were."

"Was she pretty?" Selina ventured to ask, her eyes twinkling.

"Yes, very. At first I thought how attractive she was, but gradually I found that she had little conversation. She danced like a dream, though.

"It was very hot, so near the end of the evening I walked out into the garden for a breath of fresh air. I was looking at a fascinating old well when Felicity joined me.

"I asked how she was such a good dancer. She told me she had perfected her skills on a recent visit to France, where she had been taught by a Frenchman called Pierre, who was such an expert dancer that he had once appeared on the stage.

"After that he had earned his living by becoming a private tutor of dancing. She had taken many lessons with him and at last fell in love with him."

"How romantic!" cried Selina. "Did he fall in love with her?"

"Apparently very much so," he answered. "But her father is a Duke and the Frenchman knew that there was no chance of him ever being able to marry her."

"Did she realise?"

"Oh, yes. She realised that her father would never allow her to marry a Frenchman who earned his living by teaching young girls to dance.

"When it was time for her to return to England they declared their love, although they knew it was hopeless.

"They said goodbye to each other and she returned to England. She lived in the eye of the social whirl, going to every ball of the Season. But no partner meant anything to her because she was always thinking of Pierre.

"Oh, poor girl, I am sorry for her," said Selina. "It must be terrible to know you can never marry the man you love. I suppose it would be impossible for her to make her father change his mind."

"Completely impossible. Now I had better tell you the rest of the story. We sat for a long time at the well. I was sympathetic to Felicity, but there was nothing I could really say.

"After a long time we walked back to the house to find most of the party had gone to bed. There were only a few men having a last drink before they turned in.

"Therefore picture my amazement when her father, the Duke, then accosted me and accused me of ruining his daughter's reputation.

"I apologised and explained she was only telling me about her visit to Paris. But he insisted that everyone had been scandalised by our being out there so long and he only hoped I had 'behaved myself decently' and asked her to be my wife."

Selina gave a gasp.

"Did he really say that?" she asked, astounded.

"Yes, he did. I couldn't think what to say. It had never struck me for a moment that anyone would consider it extraordinary, since we were sitting in the open air and could be seen clearly from the house and by anyone else in the garden."

"What else did he say?"

"He told me again that it was my duty to propose and 'save her reputation'."

"And what did you do?"

A glimmer of humour flickered in his eyes.

"I asserted myself."

"How?" she asked hopefully.

"I told him that he was talking nonsense and went to bed. I know this will probably strike you as feeble, but it was the best I could think of on the spur of the moment. I hoped it would then be the end of it.

"However, I have just received a letter from him, saying that he is coming to see me tomorrow afternoon and he will expect me to 'behave like a gentleman'.

"Otherwise he intends to go to the Queen and tell her how I have ruined his daughter's life. He feels that the Queen will insist on me not causing a scandal."

"But the Royal family has always been in the midst of scandals," said Selina sceptically. "Even I know that."

Royal scandals had been legendary since the times of the Prince Regent and had scarcely diminished when he succeeded to the throne as George IV. Since his death, three years earlier, his brother had reigned as William IV.

William's domestic life with his wife Adelaide was a model of propriety, if you ignored the ten children he had first sired by his mistress. That poor lady had been cast aside so he could settle down into marriage and with good luck father an heir.

In this he had failed. Now the country was looking to the future when his niece, the young Princess Victoria, would ascend to the throne and there would be an end to Royalty's improper ways.

"What you say is quite true," the Marquis admitted. "But Queen Adelaide is determined to bring propriety back to the Court. She fears the rise of Republican sentiment if excesses cannot be curbed, not only amongst Royalty, but among the aristocracy.

"She would not look kindly on a complaint from the Duke and he is relying on her to force my hand."

Selina gave a cry.

"How horrifying!" she exclaimed. "And why is he doing this? I simply do not understand."

The Marquis looked a little startled.

"At the risk of sounding immodest, I believe I am considered a reasonably good catch."

"But not to him, surely?"

"I beg your pardon?"

"I mean, he is a Duke, which is a peg higher than a Marquis. Surely he wants to marry Felicity off to another Duke? Or even a Royal Prince?"

"Ah, I see what you mean. A mere Marquis might be considered coming down in the world – "

"If you were a Duke, it certainly would be."

"True, but you have to consider the current state of the market," he said with apparent seriousness. "Dukes are in short supply and unmarried ones virtually non-existent. And I cannot offhand think of any unmarried Princes.

"So, in default of any better prospect he is forced to make do with just a mere Marquis. It's a great sacrifice for him, of course, but a man must do the best he can!"

Selina chuckled, appreciating the way his dry wit matched her own. She was unused to men who talked with this kind of drollery as John Gardner's friends got drunk and bawled with laughter at infantile jokes.

"Well you must not give in. Not just for your own sake, but for hers. How can this poor girl marry you if she loves another man?"

"Not every woman is as brave and spirited as you," the Marquis observed. "She would never dare run away."

"I suppose *you* could run away," suggested Selina, "but you'd have to hurry if he is coming here tomorrow."

"I have a better idea if you will agree to it."

She looked at him in surprise.

"How do I come into it?"

"I thought that I could introduce you to him as my *fiancée!*"

At first Selina was taken aback, but then the plan appealed to her.

"I see. Yes, of course, he cannot ask you to marry his daughter if you are already promised to someone else?"

"Exactly, Selina, then he'll go away and I'll do my best not to come into contact with him in the future."

She realised he was in a tight corner and she could not see any other way out for him.

And why should she not help him? Her own best safety might lie in remaining here for a day or two.

The Marquis was now looking at her almost with an expression of pleading in his eyes.

"I promise you that no one will know what we tell the Duke. He isn't likely to talk about it and all we have to do is lie low until it is all forgotten."

Selina took a deep breath.

"All right. If you really think it will help you, I will agree that we are engaged."

A light came into the Marquis's eyes.

"Thank you, thank you. It is an awful thing to ask someone to do, but it could solve the problem for both of us. Neither of us wants to be forced into a marriage with somebody we do not love."

"I agree. I always believed I would find someone to love, as my mother loved my father, and he would love me

38

in the same way. I will not settle for anything less and nor must you."

"I don't intend to," he asserted. "However long it takes. And it may take a very long time indeed. I've been rather slow in looking round for a wife, because there are women who will marry me for the title alone and that is not what I want. I've even thought perhaps I'll never marry."

"For shame, sir," she teased. "Have you no thought for your family?"

"Oh, the line itself is safe enough. I have a younger brother who already has a wife and two sons. I consider it absolves me from all responsibility."

"Now that was a very unwise thing to say!"

"You think it's tempting fate?" he asked anxiously.

"Worse still, it's tempting young ladies who cannot bear to see a man go free. If I was like them, I would tilt my lance at you now, not because you are a Marquis, but because you have just proclaimed your independence and I just could not resist the challenge!"

He frowned as if he was considering her seriously.

"But you don't think you would be likely to do so?"

"It wouldn't be fair since we are working as a team now. Besides, I might fail, and that would put me in a bad temper."

"Which would be very inconvenient, I do see."

"We must concentrate entirely on our chief aim," insisted Selina with a touch of sternness. "No distractions or else – disaster."

"Agreed. So let us be practical. I can give you my mother's engagement ring to wear. I have a portrait of her wearing the very ring. Come, I'll show you."

He seized her hand and hurried unceremoniously out of the room and into the library.

"There!" he cried, pointing to the wall.

The portrait was of a beautiful woman with her arm resting on a table and her engagement ring clearly visible.

"I will bring the Duke in here. You will sit near the picture and we'll make certain he notices the ring. Why are you laughing? Have I said something funny?"

"Not at all. It's merely that you are so changed suddenly. You were so quiet and grave and now you are like a jumping bean!"

He grinned.

"It wasn't very polite of me to haul you away like that, was it? I am sorry. It must be the effect you have on me. You are a bit like a jumping bean yourself!"

"I am?"

"What other young lady would brave the world as you have done. My dear, I am so glad we have met. I was feeling a little depressed before you flamed into my life."

"Even before the Duke's letter?"

"Yes, even before that. For some reason everything around me seemed dull and conventional. But who could feel like that with you around?

"Now I think the most sensible thing we can do is to go to bed and get a good night's sleep to be fresh for the trials that will face us tomorrow. I usually go for a ride in the early morning. Would you care to join me?"

Selina's eyes lit up.

"On one of your marvellous horses?" she enquired.

"My stables are at your disposal, ma'am."

Selina laughed.

"Oh, how I wish that was true."

"*If wishes were horses, beggars might ride,*" the Marquis quoted and she laughed again.

"I'll tell Mrs. Musgrove to have you called at seven thirty unless it is too early for you."

"That will be perfect."

They went into the Great Hall. The candles which they were to take upstairs were alight and standing in gold holders at the bottom of the stairs.

"How delightful," Selina exclaimed, picking up her candle. "I am so glad your house is lit with candles. It is much more romantic than the gaslight that, unfortunately, we have in my home."

"Then I am glad I can offer you something better," the Marquis replied as they started up the stairs together.

When they reached the first landing he turned to the right and Selina turned to the left.

"Goodnight," she called, "and as Mama always said to me, God bless you."

"Good night and I think you are simply wonderful," answered the Marquis.

"I hope you will think so tomorrow," smiled Selina. "But we must wait and see."

Carrying her light, she went to her bedroom, which was only a little way down the passage.

Her nightdress was lying on the bed and there were candles flickering on each side of the dressing table.

For a moment she stared at herself in the mirror.

Then she grinned.

'Who would have thought that a day which began so badly could end like this?'

She said her prayers as her mother had taught her and then she snuggled down and closed her eyes.

'I have been so very lucky,' she mused. 'I can only hope it will continue. And I want the Marquis to be lucky too, because he is so nice and I want him to find his ideal. Now, I wonder exactly what his ideal would be – '

She tried to conjure up such a perfect woman, but her eyes were heavy and in a few moments she fell asleep and slept peacefully without dreaming until morning.

*

True to his promise, he sent the housekeeper for her early and she was dressed and in the stables almost as soon as he was himself.

He wore plain clothes that, though neat and clean, looked as though he had owned them a long time. And the grey horse he rode was powerful but not elegant.

It was all a part of the man, she thought. Nothing about him was just for show. Everything fine was hidden within, only to be revealed to those he trusted.

The pretty little white mare he had chosen for her almost made her cry out with joy.

"She is a very gentle soul," explained the Marquis, "because I didn't know how spirited you like your mount to be, although I would guess you prefer a lively animal."

"True," Selina laughed, "but this lady is perfect."

"But I am right about you being a daring rider?"

"When I am allowed to be. My stepfather thinks ladies should only ride sleepy donkeys, so that's what he keeps in the stables. Which means that you only have my word for my riding ability."

"I would believe your word before anyone. Strange though it seems, I would know if you were lying. Except that I believe lying would be impossible to you."

"How would you know?"

"I am not certain. But there is something about you which makes me sure that you are speaking the truth. Not only about your riding, but everything else you say. And that is rare these days."

"Why?" enquired Selina.

"Because many will lie simply to obtain what they want or because they are pretending to be better than they are. But not you. I don't think you are capable of a single insincere thought or feeling."

It was a very strange compliment, but it pleased her more than all the flattery in the world. The Marquis was so unusual and so different from anyone she had ever met that she would like him to believe in her.

"Are you ready for what faces us today?" he asked as they cantered over his estate.

"I hope so. We are going to need our wits about us and I am already sending a prayer up to Heaven for help."

The Marquis looked at her quizzically.

"Is that what you usually do?"

"Of course. Who can possibly help me better than the angels in Heaven and all those who loved us when they were on earth?"

She spoke seriously and he replied,

"I might well have guessed you would say that. It is what makes you so unlike anyone else."

"Perhaps you would think it strange of me to talk about Heaven. But you too are unlike others and I find I always say what I think."

"And I hope you will always do so with me. But it can be dangerous. Many people just cannot cope with too much honesty!"

"I know," she sighed absently, "and what I think isn't always what I should say."

"Well, I want the truth and only the truth. It is what makes a real friendship between two people.

43

"I wouldn't say this to anyone else," he added after a moment, "but I know I can trust you. Another reason why I could never marry Lady Felicity is because she's a ninny! A charming, sweet-natured ninny with nothing in her head.

"In fact, that is really why our conversation took so long. She will insist on saying everything three times and going off at tangents. While listening to the details of her thwarted love, I also learned about her grandfather's gout, the laziness of their cook and the disgusting habits of her aunt's cat!"

Selina gave a choke of laughter.

"And if you wanted to be a clergyman, I daresay you are fond of books and serious discussions."

"Precisely. The poor girl would find me as great a disaster as a husband as I would find her as a wife."

They rode on.

After breakfast he showed her the house, including the long picture gallery where his ancestors gazed down.

There was the Marquis's father, staring out of the canvas with an air of arrogance and there was his mother, looking sweet and gentle, her daughters beside her and a little boy at her feet.

"That is my younger brother Simon. He is grown up now, of course, and lives in London with his family."

"And this – " Selina asked, moving onto the next portrait, "must be Jack."

He was exactly as the Marquis had described, a big, muscular man who looked as though he rode at life with a whoop. He would drink, laugh and romp in the hay with any willing girl. But his roistering was tempered by a kind heart. All this she could see in his portrait.

"He looks such fun," she breathed. "I wish I had known him."

"I knew you would say that. You would have liked him. Everyone loved him for miles around."

"My Lord  – "

"Ian," he said immediately. "You must get into the habit of calling me Ian if we are to seem convincing.

"Well, Selina, it's almost luncheon time, so let us eat heartily and keep up our strength. Then we will be well prepared for when the villain makes his appearance."

# CHAPTER FOUR

When they met again over luncheon, the Marquis had changed into the kind of elegant clothes that would be expected for a gentleman of his rank.

Selina had changed into the fluffiest prettiest gown she possessed.

"I couldn't decide what kind of appearance to put in, so I thought I should be faintly silly."

"Why?"

"A woman can get away with an awful lot if men think she's a fool. Take my word for it, Ian."

His lips twitched

"I bow to your expertise, ma'am – Selina. And of course you are right. We have to do this properly. Would you object if I was to hold your hand in front of the Duke?"

"I should not object at all," she smiled.

"And – er – the odd casual endearment? All in the interests of accuracy, of course?"

"We *must* be accurate at all costs," she agreed.

He took her hand in his.

For a moment Selina thought that he was practising 'accuracy', but then he produced a ring from his pocket.

"Your hand is just the same size as my mother's," he commented. "And her ring will fit you perfectly."

He slid it onto the third finger of her left hand and Selina regarded it with awe.

The picture had not done justice to this exquisite creation of diamonds and emeralds.

She had never seen anything so beautiful.

"It fits you perfectly," he said in a quiet voice.

"I'll take the greatest care of it," she promised, "and then give it back to you."

For a minute he seemed to be deep in a dream.

"What did you say?" he enquired.

"I'll give it back to you – when the Duke leaves."

He appeared to shake himself.

"Ah, yes – give it back to me. Yes."

A noise from outside the room made him snatch his hand away from her just before the butler entered with the first course.

They spoke little during the luncheon. Their minds were on the difficult afternoon to come.

As soon as they had finished, the Marquis led the way to the library and indicated for Selina to sit near to his mother's portrait.

They were only just in time.

The next moment the butler appeared to announce,

"His Grace the Duke of Wendover, my Lord."

Selina drew in her breath.

This was it.

As the Duke walked into the library, she sent up a prayer that she and the Marquis might be successful.

The Marquis advanced towards the Duke.

"Good afternoon," he greeted him. "I hope you did not have any difficulty in finding your way here."

"I have been here before," the Duke answered in a rather harsh voice. Plainly he was not going to waste time on polite chatter.

Looking at him, Selina thought that he was exactly the sort of bully she had expected him to be. He had a red plump face with small piggy eyes, gleaming with a cold determination to have his own way. If he did not get it, it was clear that he would be very unpleasant.

His eyes flickered over the room until they came to rest on Selina and they grew smaller with suspicion.

The Marquis shook hands with the Duke and said,

"Let me introduce you to Lady Selina Napier."

"How do you do?" the Duke snapped. He looked menacingly at the Marquis.

"I wish to see you alone."

"There is no need as I have no secrets from Lady Selina."

The Duke looked at her sharply and she simpered.

"I think this is one matter you will want to hear in private."

Selina reached up to take her *fiancé's* hand, in such a way that her own hand, displaying the engagement ring, was clearly visible.

"Is he going to be violent?" she asked, adding for good measure, " – dearest."

"Of course not, my love," said the Marquis, patting her hand reassuringly. "Nobody is going to be violent."

"Violence makes me so nervous, as you know."

"Madam – " the Duke growled irritably.

"Of course I realise that some gentlemen are prone to violence and I'm sure it's not to be wondered at," Selina twittered. "They lead such difficult lives, do they not?"

"Madam – "

"I am certain no lady could endure it for a moment and that is why – "

"*Madam!*"

Selina gave a little scream.

"Oh, he is being violent. Protect me, dearest."

"Let me handle this, my dear," said the Marquis, who sounded as though he was having difficulty speaking.

"Wendover, I am afraid that you have discovered our secret. Lady Selina has honoured me by consenting to become my wife."

*"She has what?"* the Duke demanded.

"We are engaged. At last I've found her, the perfect woman, the perfect Marchioness of Castleton. Won't you be the first to congratulate me?"

The Duke stared at him out of eyes that had grown very hard.

Then the Marquis added quickly,

"Would you like something to drink?"

"I require nothing," he replied, "but I am astonished at this news."

"Astonished that I have found a lady to put up with me?" asked the Marquis smoothly. "I'm a little astonished myself. But my darling is a very brave young woman – "

His darling tittered.

"Sir, you should be ashamed of yourself!" the Duke thundered. "This woman is a hussy!"

"What?" the Marquis stared at him.

"Do you think I don't know that she is an actress, hired to fob me off so you can get out of doing your duty?"

"This," the Marquis now thundered, "is Lady Selina Napier, daughter of Lord Napier, who you have probably heard of."

That stopped the Duke in his tracks.

However angry he might be, he was aware that the Marquis would never take such a risk as claiming a false identity for his fiancée, knowing how easily he could be discovered.

"I am awaiting your apology to Lady Selina," said the Marquis quietly.

"I apologise," the Duke barked. "I misunderstood. You, madam, have my sympathy."

Selina took her face out of her dainty handkerchief, where she had buried it on being called a hussy.

"Oh, but you are mistaken," she came in earnestly. "I assure you I need no sympathy. It is a very good match. All my friends have said so, and look, already my dear one has given me his mother's ring."

She extended her hand so that it flashed in the light.

"Aren't I a lucky girl?" she sighed.

The Marquis turned away, covering his eyes in an attempt to control his twitching lips.

"You may think you are lucky," the Duke growled. "But I know differently. This is a man without honour, madam. He has made love to my daughter, damaged her reputation and refused to do the decent thing."

"For pity's sake, Wendover, stop talking nonsense," the Marquis begged him in disgust. "Your daughter and I merely held a long conversation. There was no secrecy, and anyone who wanted to could have joined in. In fact, when I told my fiancée that you considered I had ruined your daughter's reputation, she laughed at the idea."

"That's true, I did," Selina agreed earnestly.

"She said," the Marquis continued, "that if every man was made to marry a woman he had talked to in an open garden, there would be countless more marriages and most of them would be miserable."

"You may be making a joke of the whole matter," the Duke spat back angrily, "but I consider your behaviour disgraceful. You talked with her for hours – "

"Wendover, I must point out that the length of the conversation was due mainly to Lady Felicity's tendency to – " here the Marquis's good manners clashed with his need to be plain, " – to speak at length," he finished.

The Duke snorted with disgust.

"If you are trying to tell me that my daughter is a fool, who does not believe she's made her point until she's made it ten times, then say so. It's no secret to me. Lord knows I have put up with it for long enough – in her, in her mother, in every woman of the wretched family. Idiots, all of them. But what does that have to do with marriage?"

"It might have a lot to do with it if a man was not of a very patient disposition," observed the Marquis. "Besides which a husband likes to get a word in, now and then."

"Well, when you are married you can order her to shut up," the Duke snapped. "Not that that ever did me much good, but you might be luckier.

"There's no doubt in my mind, whatever you may say, that you have damaged my daughter's future and she is entitled to become your wife."

"With the very best will in the world," the Marquis replied lightly, "I find it impossible to have two wives. As Lady Selina has promised to marry me, I can hardly ask your daughter to accompany her up the aisle!

"Unless of course we move to one of those foreign countries where a man can take several wives. You would not mind that, would you, dearest?"

Selina now rose to her feet, clasped her hands on her breast and declared melodramatically,

"I will follow you anywhere in the world, darling."

"No doubt you think it is clever to make a joke of this," the Duke fumed. "If I was younger and stronger I'd call you out."

"Out?" Selina asked, wide-eyed. "Out where?"

"Don't tell her for pity's sake!" snarled the Duke, "or we'll have her in hysterics again."

"Out where?" asked Selina again.

"Never mind where, madam. There's nothing more to say, except that this whole situation is a disgrace."

"But out *where*?" demanded Selina.

"It's all right, my beloved," the Marquis interrupted soothingly. "The Duke wants to fight a duel and blow my brains out."

Selina screamed and fainted into his arms.

The Duke scowled at them both wrathfully before storming out.

Neither of them moved an inch until they had heard the front door close.

Without opening her eyes, Selina asked,

"Has he really gone?"

"Yes, it is all right."

She opened one eye, full of amusement. Slowly the Marquis straightened, drawing her upright.

He could have released her, but he kept his arms about her until he was quite sure she was steady.

Suddenly his heart soared as it had not done for so many years and at exactly the same second they both began to laugh.

"You should have seen his face!" he choked.

"I wish I had, but I had to keep my eyes closed. It's not fair that you should have all the fun."

"Fun? I don't know when I've been through such a nerve-wracking experience. I have aged at least ten years. Oh, Selina, Selina, what you put me through!"

"I warned you I was going to be silly."

"That performance was a good deal more than silly. I didn't know where to look – his face when you – "

But laughter overcame him and he could say no more.

He tightened his arms and suddenly her own arms were about his neck. They clung together, rocking back and forth in an agony of mirth.

"You were marvellous," he crowed. "Wonderful."

"So were you," she chuckled. "Oh, Ian – Ian – "

He looked straight into her face, and suddenly self-consciousness swept over him. He released her hastily, and she, also self-conscious, stepped back.

"Yes, it went well, didn't it?"

Selina nodded.

"He was really taken aback when you forced him to apologise to me."

"Of course," he muttered, his face suddenly dark. "How dare he!"

"Don't be cross," she begged. "I have never been called a hussy before – it's the first time!"

He grinned unwillingly.

"It's good of you to take it so well. I had no right to expose you to insult. Thank goodness it's all over."

Her laughter died.

"I'm not sure that it is. I saw the malevolence in his eyes. He is not going to leave matters there."

That checked him.

"You are right, of course."

"Ian, I think you'd be wise to do what I have done."

The Marquis stared at her.

"Are you suggesting that I should run away?"

"Why not?" Selina questioned. "The world is a big place and if you were away just a short time, he can shout and scream all he likes. People will forget and talk about something else."

"You are right. But you must come with me."

"What are you saying?"

"We'll have to stay together for a month or two at least. Otherwise he'll guess the truth and go to the Queen."

"You must not let him do so. You are right, Ian, we will both fight this together and stand 'shoulder to shoulder against the advancing foe'."

Impulsively he seized her hands in his.

"It must have been my guardian angel who sent me out last night to find you."

"And my guardian angel too," she agreed. "They were working as a team."

"And we too must work as a team," he mused. "I have it. My yacht is at Portsmouth. We should now go abroad, perhaps for a month or two. As you say, after a while they will find something else to talk about."

"Yes, but that something else will be *us*."

"How do you mean?"

"You and I, sailing away together on your yacht, will be the biggest scandal of the age."

He stopped.

"Of course. I was too distracted to think carefully. You must take a chaperone with us. Martha would be the best person, I think."

"Who is Martha?"

"She was my mother's lady's maid. Since Mama died Martha has felt a bit lost. She has worked for both my sisters, but it wasn't a success, chiefly due to her habit of quarrelling with everyone. She left both their houses in a state of high dudgeon and came back here.

"Now she has set herself to looking after me, which means she is always quarrelling with my valet, Simpkins. They will probably enliven our journey with a feud, but it cannot be helped."

A thought struck him.

"Did you bring your passport?"

"I did indeed. I had no idea where my flight might take me."

"Then the sooner we leave the better. Preferably today. If we stay three nights on the way to Portsmouth, we will arrive about midday and catch the evening tide."

*

Selina met Martha early the next morning while she was drinking the tea that the maid had brought her.

Martha was in her mid-fifties with a stern face and lofty manner. The late Marchioness of Castleton had been a lady of elegance and since her death Martha had suffered from a feeling of not being appreciated.

She looked Selina up and down balefully and then grunted approval.

"Later on I will review your Ladyship's clothes and see what must be done," she observed loftily.

She then sailed out leaving Selina wondering if she ought to curtsy.

The Marquis chuckled when she told him.

"She really terrifies me. She is deeply displeased at having to travel with Simpkins. She does concede that he knows his job, but she considers his behaviour to me is too free and easy. We shall have to try very hard to measure up to her standards."

They ate breakfast quickly and then it was time to leave. Outside Selina found a smart curricle drawn by two perfectly matched black horses.

"The fastest in my stables," the Marquis promised her. "We will need frequent changes of horses along the way, so that we reach Portsmouth as quickly as possible."

Behind the curricle came a post chaise for Martha and Simpkins. The luggage would follow in a wagon.

"You don't think that we might attract unwelcome attention travelling in such style?" she enquired.

"We are bound to, I am afraid. But when we reach the posting inns, Simpkins will inform anyone who cares to listen that we are a certain Mr. Pearson travelling with his sister. Anyone pursuing us will hear that story."

"Will they believe it?"

"Even if they don't, it would sow confusion which will be useful."

They both turned to look at the stately procession that emerged from the front door. First came Martha, her nose in the air.

When she reached the chaise, she stopped while a powdered footman opened the door and let down the steps. Behind her came Simpkins, a thin sharp-faced little man, several inches shorter than Martha.

Before following her into the chaise, he turned to the Marquis and gave an eloquent shrug, rolling his eyes to Heaven. Then the chaise swallowed him up.

"Madam," now invited the Marquis with an elegant flourish, indicating the curricle.

"Sir, you are too kind."

In another moment she was high up in the curricle,

gazing out over the brown shiny backs of the horses. The Marquis joined her, gave his coachman a signal to start and they were on their way.

For the first hour Selina concentrated on enjoying herself. The wind was blowing in her face, the sun was shining and above all she was free.

She kept looking anxiously over her shoulder, but as no one seemed to be following them she began to relax.

"You ought to write a book about our adventures," she told the Marquis. "It will be so incredible that it will certainly be a best-seller – and pay for all the expenses we are incurring."

"*I* am incurring," the Marquis corrected her. "Let me make it clear from the beginning that you come as my guest and you don't spend your own money on this strange and rather wild adventure."

"Oh, but I cannot allow you to buy everything for me," protested Selina. "I have money of my own."

"You keep your money. You may need it in the future. I do not allow my guests to spend their money on me and, as I am exceedingly grateful to you for saving me from a life of boredom, any money I spend is worth it for the new experience."

"You are so kind, Ian, I really do not know what to say."

"Well, whatever it is to be, make it amusing," he suggested. "I want to laugh on this journey. Too little of my life has been spent in laughter.

"Then, yesterday, you appeared, and since then I seem to be laughing all the time. That's how I want it to be. I am afraid I have become rather a dull fellow."

"Don't say that about yourself. You are not a dull fellow and besides, I expect you laughed more when you were younger."

The Marquis winced a little at this suggestion that she regarded him as a greybeard, but only replied mildly,

"I don't think I did. Except when I was with my brother, Jack. His antics were a constant entertainment, but I was frequently required to put on what Jack called my 'clerical face' to help him out of some scrape or other. I was very good at explaining him to my father."

"Accurately?"

"Good Heavens, no! If I had explained it all to him accurately he would have been in even worse trouble. No, I contrived to put a gloss on things.

"Once my father asked, 'why doesn't your brother face me himself?' But then he commented, 'of course, he doesn't have the gift of the gab, like you.' He was right.

"And then poor Jack died and there was no more laughter for any of us. I think I had forgotten how to laugh until you came to remind me how."

"What a really nice thing to say," blushed Selina. "Perhaps you could put that comment in the book."

"No," answered the Marquis after a while. "I don't think I would like anyone else to read it." He sounded a little apologetic. "I am afraid you will think it very poor spirited of me."

"Oh no," Selina responded kindly. "We cannot put in everything or it will sound too fantastic."

"I think what is happening to me *is* fantastic. But I am very willing to allow it to happen," he murmured, but so quietly that Selina did not hear him.

"We don't want people to think it is an invention from the beginning to the end," she pointed out.

"Wait just a moment!" he exclaimed. "We haven't reached the end yet. It might be marvellous, as we both hope or it might be disastrous."

"I am quite sure it will be marvellous both for you and for me."

"I sincerely hope it will be marvellous for *you*," he said fervently. "In fact, I really hope you have everything you want in your life."

There was an intense note in his voice she had not heard before and which left her floundering for an answer. While she was still thinking, he turned his attention back to the horses and seemed to forget all about her.

Just before six o'clock they reached the small town of Eppingham.

"I have heard there's a good posting inn here," said the Marquis. "*The Belfry*. There it is."

They drove into the yard. An ostler came bustling out, rubbing his hands at the prospect of so many horses staying the night.

"I promise you, sir, they'll be very comfortable," he called. "As the inn has recently been refurbished, you'll be comfortable too."

The Marquis helped Selina out of the carriage and they walked into the inn, which was indeed well-furnished and agreeable.

The Marquis strode up to the desk and introduced himself as Mr. Pearson, travelling with his sister.

He required a single room for himself, a double for his sister and her companion and something for Simpkins and the two drivers.

An elderly woman took them upstairs and showed them two bedrooms close to each other, looking out over the garden at the back of the inn.

"I can promise you, sir, it's nice and quiet 'ere."

"Then we are so lucky to find this inn," the Marquis

answered, "and the rooms look very comfortable. Well, my dear sister, I'll leave you to get ready for dinner."

With Martha's help Selina changed from her riding habit into a gown that was pretty but simple and not costly enough to attract attention.

Eventually the Marquis came to knock on her door and they went down to a small elegant dining room.

They sat together at a table for two, while at some way off Martha, Simpkins and the drivers dined together.

Feeling in a festive mood the Marquis invited them to join his table, but the four servants were shocked at this breach of protocol.

They thanked him and then declined so loftily that he was made aware that he had offended against decorum.

"That has put me in my place," he observed wryly. "I'm afraid I've lost their good opinion entirely. Whatever shall I do?"

Selina giggled.

"It's probably just as well. Martha and Simpkins are working up to another argument."

They glanced over to the other table where Martha and Simpkins were talking to each other in airs of haughty politeness, while the two drivers looked on as if it was all too much to bear.

It was an excellent meal and the Marquis very soon proposed an early night.

"Then we can be away quickly in the morning."

He escorted Selina and Martha to the door of their room.

"If you are frightened or if anything upsets you in the night, you know you have only to call for me."

"Thank you, Ian. That is so reassuring."

"Her Ladyship will be perfectly all right with me," Martha insisted repressively.

"I am sure she will be," the Marquis agreed with a meekness that made Selina give a little choke of laughter.

He looked at her with appreciation.

"Goodnight, Selina."

"Goodnight, Ian."

Once in bed she said her prayers and thanked God for helping her to find someone so kind and helpful as the Marquis.

'I like him very very much,' she told herself. 'And he is far too nice to be forced into marriage with someone he does not love.'

She prayed that he would be happy, then fell asleep still thinking about him.

# CHAPTER FIVE

Selina was up early next morning.

After all the exertions of yesterday, she was feeling hungry and enjoyed the eggs and bacon and ripe fruit that was waiting for them.

"I just cannot wait to see your yacht," she remarked breezily.

"I promise you, it is very up-to-date," the Marquis told her. "Everyone who has travelled in it admires it and most of them try to rename it."

He laughed as he added,

"It is called *The Mermaid*, but I think we will have to change the name to *The Selina*."

She considered this idea and then shook her head.

"That doesn't sound at all like a yacht. I think you should call it the name of your wife, when you find her."

"I didn't think of that," he replied. "I wonder if it would really be a sensible thing to do."

Selina laughed.

"It depends on you. If you're going to change your wife so often, it will be a serious nuisance having to paint out one name and putting on another!"

The Marquis grinned.

"And just how would I go about changing my wife very often?"

She shrugged airily.

"Bluebeard managed it!"

"Bluebeard didn't live in England."

"It wouldn't have made any difference if he had," she replied, refusing to admit defeat. "He would have done just what he liked anywhere."

"And you suggest I follow his example?"

"Not at all, I think you should avoid his example. Otherwise, you will always be renaming your yacht!"

He shouted out with laughter, so that everyone else in the breakfast room stared at them.

"Just when I believe I know you," he chortled, "you manage to come out with something totally unexpected,"

"I am glad, because if you thought I was repeating myself too often, you might put me off at the first country we come to and I would have to find my way back home by swimming!"

"A fine opinion you have of me, ma'am! Do you really think I could do such a thing?"

"No, I think that you are just much too kind and understanding of other's feelings. The reason you are here is because you were sorry for someone and listened to her troubles for too long."

He nodded wryly.

"I am being punished for being a fool and there is no other word for it."

"No, you are not a fool, just a very kind man."

"Thank you, but sometimes I wonder if there is any difference."

"Of course there is. I hope you never give up being kind, but I don't believe you will, because that is the man you are."

He gave his delightful smile.

"Does that mean I will have to spend the rest of my life running away in a curricle?"

"I suppose it might," she replied in a teasing voice.

"Well, I don't mind as long as you are with me."

Before she could answer, he added hastily,

"Now, if you have finished, we should be going."

Once the Marquis had paid the inn's bill and tipped everyone generously, they went outside to where Martha and Simpkins were waiting to board the chaise.

They had stopped quarrelling and were pointedly ignoring each other.

The Marquis grinned.

"Let them sort it out their own way."

He helped her aboard the curricle, Lovall got into the driver's seat and Wilkins mounted the wagon.

At a signal from the Marquis, they all set off.

"So far, so good," he said as they passed out of the narrow lanes and on to the main road.

"Cross your fingers, Ian, I won't feel really happy until I am at sea."

She looked up at the sunny sky and breathed a sigh of pleasure.

"What a lovely day! I even feel as though I might miss England. I know when I went to Finishing School in France, it took me a week or so to stop thinking about the dogs and horses I had left behind me and begin to enjoy the French with all their wit, all their jokes and above all their compliments."

"Which you have in abundance, Selina."

"Not all that many but I do have some. Englishmen seldom say really nice things in case you either laugh at them or take them too seriously."

"That is so true," agreed the Marquis. "I remember Jack saying he would never dare praise a girl's looks too extravagantly in case she thought he was proposing."

"And now you have just found the same except that you didn't even have to pay a compliment!"

"Indeed."

"But you need not worry," she said impishly. "You can pay me any number of compliments and I promise not to sue you for breach of promise!"

He chuckled.

"That does relieve my mind, ma'am."

"I thought it would," she added demurely.

It was an energetic day for the Marquis kept up a swift pace. Several times they stopped at post houses for a change of horses and once they lingered for a long lunch. But then they were off again.

Wherever they stopped Selina would scan the road behind them, but there was never anything to alarm her.

At seven o'clock that evening they pulled into *The Three Bells* at Picthaven, a small but prosperous town.

The inn was considerably more luxurious than their previous accommodation, but there was a tense atmosphere which was soon traced to the landlord.

He was a young man built like a bull with a face that could have been handsome if he was not so sullen.

Selina guessed that he was a favourite with young women, but he had eyes only for one. This was a young woman of luscious appearance who seemed about to burst out of her dress. Martha sniffed when she saw her.

The girl showed them to their rooms and swore she was ready to do anything to ensure their comfort. Selina noticed that, as she said this, she made eyes at the Marquis.

At least, she thought so. It was hard to be sure as the girl had a pronounced squint.

It might have been expected that a Marquis would greet these overtures with a lofty disdain, but instead, he thanked her politely and gave her a charming smile which made her ogle him even more.

Of course, Selina quietly reasoned, the Marquis was the most courteous man in the world.

But courtesy could be taken too far.

Selina took a lot of trouble over her appearance that night. The previous night she had chosen a dress that was pretty but simple.

Tonight she chose one of her most elegant gowns, a creation of honey-coloured silk slightly low in the front and with it she wore a necklace of garnets.

"Shall I do your hair properly tonight, my Lady?" asked Martha, who had been most offended the previous evening when Selina had refused to allow her to dress her hair elegantly.

"Yes, please Martha," Selina consented decidedly.

They were both pleased with the result.

Selina's lovely fair hair was amassed on her head in a riot of delicate curls, except for the odd stray tresses that were allowed to fall elegantly down her long neck and onto her shoulder.

As she descended the stairs the Marquis's eyes told her that she was indeed beautiful.

He was stylishly dressed as well with a cravat that must have taken all Simpkins's skill to make perfect.

"You are quite right," he said, as he handed her to her chair. "It is too easy to let standards slip when we are travelling. But you and I will not fall into that trap."

"No, I do agree," she replied. "Not even when we are on your yacht, which I hope we will be very soon."

"The night we left I had sent a rider on ahead with a letter to my Captain telling him to be prepared for us. He should be well ahead of us by now and with luck we will arrive to find him ready to cast off as soon as we're aboard.

"So, all is being done as speedily as possible, but, I will concur, it would be nice to move faster."

"If only we could go by train," sighed Selina.

The Marquis grinned.

"What do you know about trains?"

"Just that as everyone will know, the first passenger service was opened three years ago between Manchester and Liverpool and it has been such a success that railways are being built all over the country as fast as possible."

"What a very well informed young lady you are."

"Well, you can thank my stepfather," she admitted. "He never stops talking about trains and what a scandal it is that they do not run as far as Portsmouth yet. He thinks it would improve his business."

"So he discusses such matters with you?"

"Not at all. He just makes speeches. He does not care who's listening, but there needs to be someone, so that he is not actually talking to himself. I will do, if he cannot find anyone better."

"So, one way and another you have learned quite a lot about railways?"

"I think they are really exciting."

"They are the future. Just think of being able to make a journey in just a few hours, instead of a few days. Never mind. We will do the best we can.

"Everything should be ready the moment we arrive at the quay and we will head straight for Gibraltar, then the

Mediterranean. Apart from that, we have not yet decided on where to go. Do you have any wishes?"

"Only to be away safely."

"That's what I wish too, but it's not a destination. After Gibraltar – where? Spain? Italy?"

"Have you been to those countries?"

"I have travelled a little."

"Tell me about them, please."

He began to talk, creating bright exotic pictures.

Selina listened, entranced.

Now there was time to consider him and appreciate what a very attractive man he really was. Until now he had been mainly just her rescuer.

It was true that she had noticed his other attributes, such as his quiet deep voice and the charming gentleness of his manners.

It was delightful to have leisure to appreciate him.

This was a man who would inspire interest from so many women, not just chambermaids. In fact, she thought, any female would be flattered to be sitting here with him, knowing that his whole attention was devoted to her.

And enjoying every moment of it.

To finish the meal he ordered champagne.

"To celebrate the start of our great adventure," he proposed. "May it bring us both all we want in life!"

"That is so delightful," sighed Selina. "But I only know what I want now. I don't think I know everything I want in life. Do you?"

"Oh yes," he responded to her quietly. "*I know*."

He finished his champagne.

"It's time for bed. Tomorrow will be a busy day."

He looked round the room, which was now empty, but for themselves. "Where is Martha?"

"She and Simpkins have probably gone outside to squabble in peace," suggested Selina.

"Again? Oh well, if it keeps them happy."

"Happy?"

"Yes, I don't think they really take it seriously. It's more of a way of passing the time. Let's go and see if we can keep them from each other's throats!"

They strolled out into the garden and immediately became aware of a commotion.

A crowd had gathered to watch something that was causing everyone to laugh and cheer. After working their way to the front, Selina and the Marquis saw what it was.

From somewhere Simpkins had found a huge cart-horse and was riding him bareback round the yard, urging the beast to jump benches. As he rode he yelped "tallyho!" He was clearly not sober.

"What the devil does he think he's playing at?" the Marquis demanded, astounded.

"Oh, my Lord, please stop him!"

This wail came from Martha who was alternately watching the performance and burying her face in a large handkerchief.

"What is the matter with him, Martha?"

"Strong drink," Martha asserted in high dudgeon. "Drink is the cause, my Lord. He was plied with alcoholic beverages by a hussy."

"Another hussy? There must be a lot of us about," Selina murmured in the Marquis's ear and he chuckled.

Under his kindly questioning Martha told a tale of passion and betrayal, which roughly translated as Simpkins accepting powerful liquor from the barmaid, who had been driven beyond reason by his manly charms.

Her attempts to seduce him had been thwarted by Martha's intercession, which had led to yet another of their arguments, even livelier than usual.

The landlord had taken a hand, resulting in a four-way exchange of pleasantries.

Quite how this had finished with Simpkins riding a carthorse around the yard nobody could quite explain. But it had certainly done so.

"Simpkins," called the Marquis. "Stop acting the fool and come back here."

"Later, my Lord," he yelled in tipsy defiance. "I'll show that fat barrel of lard who's a yellow-bellied – "

The end of the insult would never to be known, for at that moment Simpkins found himself facing a fence and made the mistake of trying to urge the horse over it. The animal sensibly refused, but it was too late for Simpkins to stop and he went sailing over the beast's head and then the fence to land on a pile of logs on the far side.

Martha screamed.

Everyone else ran forward to enjoy the spectacle. Somebody took charge of the horse which stood breathing heavily, but otherwise content to have had his fun.

The Marquis leapt over the fence to find Simpkins groaning on the ground.

"Help me bring him inside," he called.

Between them they carried the wounded Simpkins up the stairs to his room. Selina followed with Martha now weeping loudly.

"Oh Eddie," she cried, "Eddie – my Eddie – "

"*Your* Eddie?" asked Selina, mystified.

"Yes, my Lady. Oh, I know that he's a miserable, good-for-nothing layabout without any brains, but he's still *mine*. And I won't have some scruffy barmaid thinking she can push me out – saying he gave her the eye – poof! "

"I am sure he didn't," said Selina soothingly.

"Of course he didn't," Martha declared indignantly. "What sort of a man do you take my Eddie for?"

"Well, I don't know him very well."

"He's a fine man – "

"Except for being a miserable and good-for-nothing layabout?" Selina could not resist adding.

"That has nothing to do with it, my Lady. We have been true to each other these many years."

"But why didn't you marry?"

"I could never have ever put anyone before the late Marchioness."

"But after she died?"

"Eddie had all his duties," Martha asserted vaguely. "We drifted apart."

She began to sob loudly.

"Oh Eddie, don't die."

"I don't think he is in any danger of dying, Martha, judging by the curses he was uttering as they carried him to his bed!"

Selina was correct.

The doctor was swiftly summoned and pronounced that Simpkins' leg was indeed broken, but he had sustained no further hurt.

"Which does leave us in a pickle," the Marquis told her. "Obviously he cannot continue on the journey and he ought to remain here until he is well enough to be moved back home. But the landlord isn't very happy about it."

"Is he the 'fat barrel of lard' who called Simpkins a 'yellow-bellied' – ?"

"Yes, that's him. His name is Brendan and I gather he is jealous about the fair Gladys."

"And who is Gladys?"

"The barmaid."

"But she's got a squint."

"I know, but, if you disregard it, she also has ample charms, which I would not describe to a lady."

"Most wise," she agreed, beginning to understand how Martha felt.

"In addition Brendan has his eye firmly on Gladys and refuses to allow her to nurse Simpkins 'in his bed' as he puts it. I am not sure where else she could nurse him, but Brendan is determined that she is not going to. I doubt too if she has any nursing skills nor does there seem to be a good local woman I can hire."

A cold hand clutched Selina's stomach.

"We cannot simply abandon him here?"

"I know. It is not immediately clear to me what we are going to do, but it won't be that."

Even as he spoke there was a squawk from above and Simpkins' door opened and the lusty Gladys emerged so quickly that it was clear she had been propelled by some powerful force from behind.

The force turned out to be not Brendan but Martha.

"Get out of here, you trollop," she yelled.

"I was only – "

"I know what you were *only* doing and if I catch you again, I'll make you squint on the other side too!"

"Martha?" the Marquis questioned, puzzled.

In a whisper Selina gave him a hasty description of her conversation with Martha.

"You were right, Ian, they are not really enemies at all. She is just cross because she cannot pin him down to a date."

"But I never imagined anything like that."

"What on earth can be a-goin' on 'ere?" called out Brendan, entering the fray.

"Keep her out," shouted Martha. "Nobody comes in here but me."

"Suits me," growled Brendan.

He pushed past them to climb the stairs and storm into Simpkins's room.

"The sooner you're out of 'ere the better," he raged.

"Well he isn't going anywhere," screamed Martha, "he's not fit to be moved and if you try it you'll have me to reckon with."

"You?" sneered Brendan. "And *who* are you?"

"She is his fiancée," piped up Selina.

Of all her listeners it would be hard to say who was the most startled. Brendan looked at everyone with equal suspicion. Martha stared at Selina with a light dawning in her eyes.

The Marquis also stared at her, but the light in his eyes was admiration and he seemed to be seeing her for the first time.

Simpkins merely opened and closed his mouth.

"Is this true?" Brendan demanded.

"Oh, yes," Selina assured him. "They have been true to each other for years."

"Then why aren't they wed?"

"Martha had her duties with the late Marchioness," Selina recited, "and Simpkins is devoted to his Lordship."

She indicated the Marquis who was admirably swift to take up the cue.

"An excellent valet," he responded solemnly. "But Simpkins, duty and devotion can only be taken so far."

"My Lord – "

"You have sacrificed yourself enough. So I hereby free you to marry the woman you love. I shall, of course, provide your bride with a dowry and the two of you shall have a cottage on the estate."

Simpkins opened his mouth again to speak and then he met Martha's eye.

The Marquis turned to Brendan.

"Surely we could come to some arrangement?" he asked, charmingly.

"If they're a-gettin' wed, that's different. Then she can be responsible for him, and I don't want to see his face 'ere again."

After that things moved fast. The local parson was summoned and agreed that in the special circumstances he could perform the wedding here and now.

Any trouble with a Special License was taken care of by a generous donation to the Church fund.

The wedding was conducted early next morning in Simpkins's room at the inn. The Marquis was the best man and Selina the only bridesmaid.

After the Service the Marquis handed Martha a roll of banknotes amounting to two hundred pounds, which was to be her dowry.

Simpkins, lying in bed, now began to feel that there might be something to be said for matrimony after all.

"But you are to keep it," the Marquis told Martha with a wink. "Don't let this fellow get his hands on it."

"Don't you worry, my Lord, I wasn't planning to."

"And here is money for your expenses. Take good care of Simpkins and have him well for my return."

"You can safely leave everything to me, my Lord."

"But who's going to look after you now, my Lord?" Simpkins wailed. "And you, my Lady?"

"We shall just have to manage," replied Selina.

But although she spoke with assurance, she did not feel at all easy in her mind. A thought was troubling her.

The same thought had occurred to the Marquis and as soon as they had left the room he voiced it.

"The problem is," he admitted, "that this leaves the two of us travelling alone together. Which is just what we wanted to avoid. I hope I do not need to assure you that I should in all circumstances behave like a gentleman – "

"I have no doubt of that," she hurried to say.

"Thank you. That relieves my mind. Nonetheless, it's a censorious world. "

"But we cannot turn back now," she added quickly. "When you were talking to Martha, you spoke as though it was settled."

"I know, but the more I think of it, the more I can see how damaging it might be for you to travel with me without a chaperone. Your reputation would be ruined."

"I cannot go back, I just simply cannot. Anything is preferable to marrying some man forced on me by my stepfather. Even a ruined reputation."

"My dear girl, you know very little of the world if you think that. I assure you, you would not like it at all."

"I won't go back," she cried fiercely. "There must be a way. There *must* be. We will just have to find it."

There was a silence.

The Marquis was sunk in thought.

From time to time he looked at Selina cautiously, as if wondering whether he dared say what was on his mind.

At last he took a deep breath.

"Selina, you said a moment ago that you would do anything rather than go back. Did you really mean it?"

"Yes, I did, absolutely anything."

But although the words were resolute, there was a certain vagueness about her manner.

"Then I have a suggestion to make that I hope you will not find disagreeable."

He paused, waiting for Selina to ask him what his suggestion was. Now it came to the point he found himself being afraid in case she was offended. A question would have been a kind of encouragement.

But she was frowning in a distant way, as though her thoughts occupied her and he was not entirely sure that she had heard him.

"Selina," he tried again, "you must do whatever is best for you, and I would hate to think – that is, I would hate *you* to think – that I had in any way taken advantage of your position. You must tell me that you understand or I cannot say more."

"Oh yes, yes," she murmured. "I do understand."

"Because there is one way in which we can travel alone together – "

"Yes!" she agreed, suddenly alive with excitement. "Of course there is. It's been staring us in the face all this time."

"That's what I thought. I am so glad that the idea doesn't horrify you."

"Of course it doesn't. I know it's unconventional."

"But why should we care?" he asked, smiling with happiness.

"Why indeed? And besides, nobody will know."

The light died from his face.

"What did you say?"

"Nobody will know."

"But of course people will know if we're going to be mar- "

"Not if we don't tell anyone," Selina interrupted eagerly. "And, naturally, we won't. Who is to say that you didn't suddenly hire a new valet? I'll need some male clothes and I think they'll have to be new, because I'm not sure that Simpkins's clothes would fit me."

Out of all this only one word made an impact on the Marquis and it was like the tolling of a bell.

"*Valet*?" he echoed.

"Don't you think I'll make a good valet? It's lucky that I am tall and slender. This really is the ideal solution to our problem. Why, what's the matter?"

For the Marquis had begun to laugh.

"What is it?" she demanded indignantly. "Don't you think I can do it?"

"My dear, I think you can do anything in the world that you set your mind to."

"Then why are you laughing?"

"I was laughing at myself for being a fool. In fact, I am such a fool that I deserve everything I get!"

"I don't understand."

"It's probably just as well." He sighed and smiled at her. "But at least I am clever enough to know that I am a fool!"

"I wish you would stop talking in riddles," she said, rather put out.

"I'm so sorry. I promise not to do so any more. So you plan to dress up as a boy and become my valet?"

"Don't you think it's a clever notion?"

"I think it's the maddest idea I've ever heard. But I'll help you because if I don't you'll only go and think of something even more hare-brained. But where are you going to find the clothes? And how? I really don't think I can rise to the heights of buying boys' clothes."

"I'll have to ask Martha to help me. Do you think she will?"

The Marquis grinned.

"I think Martha will do anything you ask her!"

# CHAPTER SIX

As the Marquis had predicted, Martha was only too willing to help one whom she regarded as her benefactor, and when she and Selina had both climbed into the chaise, Lovall drove them off to explore the shops of Picthaven.

The Marquis remained with Simpkins to learn from him the various mysteries of valeting himself.

Although small, Picthaven was prosperous and they soon located some excellent establishments.

Selina had little experience of buying clothes as her own gowns had always been made for her by seamstresses.

She and Martha called on a tailor giving him their story about buying clothes for her brother, who was tall and slim, 'just like the lady here' as Martha expressed it.

The tailor was most anxious to help, offering to run something up in 'double-quick time'. But that turned out to mean the next day and Selina dared not wait.

But then the friendly tailor had an inspiration. It seemed that a suit had been ordered by a young gentleman who was local, liked to dress well, but did not always have the money to pay.

The tailor had adamantly refused to part with the garments except for cash, which was not forthcoming and so the clothes languished in a cupboard.

He brought them out and at once Selina knew that she had found what she was looking for. There was a pair of cream-coloured breeches and a dark blue coat with large gilt buttons worn over a gleaming white shirt.

The absent customer was evidently a dandy as the ensemble was completed by a waistcoat of dazzling design. Made of embroidered satin it was red, blue and green with a hint of glitter.

Selina eyed it ecstatically.

"Will your brother be needing boots?" enquired the tailor. "If so I can have some sent over from the boot shop just across the way."

They declared they would like to see some boots.

"And the size?" asked the tailor.

"Small," answered Martha.

"Medium," came in Selina at once.

When the tailor had departed, Martha murmured,

"If they're a man's shoes, you'll need small."

"No, I won't."

"Why ever not?"

"Because I have big feet," Selina said crossly.

The tailor returned with a large selection of shining boots only the largest of which was big enough for Selina's far from dainty feet.

When everything was chosen, the tailor enquired,

"Now, you're quite sure that the clothes will fit?"

"Not really," replied Selina. "I think I should try them on."

"*What*?"

"I mean," she amended hastily, "that my brother and I are the same size. If I can wear them, so can he."

"But the idea of a lady – "

"I know," she added sorrowfully, "but it cannot be helped. Dearest Frederick would expect me to make the sacrifice for him."

The tailor gave her a strange look and led the way to a small room at the back of the shop. Martha joined her and he departed.

"What's the matter with him?" asked Selina. "He looked as if he had seen a ghost."

"I had already told him that your brother's name is David."

Selina gave a gasp of laughter.

"Oh dear! I'm sure he thinks we are quite mad."

"And he's probably right. Let's now hurry before he sends for the Constable."

Martha helped her undress and Selina pulled on the breeches. They were tight and she saw with dismay that they hugged her figure more closely than was compatible with modesty.

Next came the shirt, followed by the waistcoat and frock coat. Finally the boots which gleamed beautifully.

She looked splendid and convincing, except for one thing.

"Your hair," groaned Martha. "You'll not manage to keep it all up, my Lady. You need a wig."

"But where am I going to find one now?"

"I saw a wig shop just up the road. We'll go there next."

Selina donned her normal clothes before returning to the tailor and informing him she would have everything.

At the wig shop fortune smiled on them. There was a gentleman's wig in Selina's own hair colour, brushed and curled in the romantic style known as *a la Titus*.

When they had purchased it, all seemed complete and by chance the wig-maker sold hats as well and Selina discovered a lovely top hat of dark brown silk that made her almost weep with pleasure. It would have been a crime not to buy it – so she did.

Finally they both piled into the chaise and returned to the inn in triumph.

There they were informed that the Marquis was still talking to Simpkins. They immediately hurried up, Martha to join her husband and Selina to slip into her room and change into her new attire, chuckling to herself.

After a few minutes she heard footsteps going past her door and down the stairs.

Looking cautiously out she saw the retreating form of the Marquis, evidently going to the tap room to fortify himself with some ale.

It took only a moment to complete her change. The wig fitted perfectly and when the dashing cloak was over her shoulders, she rammed the top hat on at a rakish angle and regarded herself in the mirror.

An elegant young gentleman with a look of impish amusement in his eyes looked out at her.

She laughed at him and he laughed back.

This was going to be fun.

She could see the Marquis as she came downstairs, standing by himself in the tap room, evidently waiting for Brendan to bring his order.

He was not looking in her direction and Selina had time to walk right down before making herself known.

When she did, it was in a raucous belligerent tone.

"Landlord! I say there, landlord!"

"He has gone to fetch some wine from the cellar," the Marquis observed, glancing over his shoulder.

Selina stayed back in the shadows and lowered her voice as much as she could manage.

"But I want to be served. I can't stand delay. Got a devilish dry throat."

"Patience, fellow, please," counselled the Marquis. "We must all wait our turn."

"Dash it man, I've no intention of waiting. That's not my way. Hallo there, landlord! Stir yourself."

The Marquis almost audibly ground his teeth.

"You compel me to remind you, sir, that I was here first."

"Pooh! Who cares for that?"

"Sir – "

Selina managed a neighing laugh, an exact copy of one she had heard from one of her stepfather's friends who was trying to appear as quality and failing miserably.

The Marquis, exasperated but unwilling to quarrel, turned away from this rude intruder.

"Don't turn your back on me, sir," hooted Selina. "Dash it all, man, do you know who I am?"

The Marquis sighed and reluctantly turned back.

"No sir, who are you?"

Selina chuckled and spoke in her own voice.

"Do you really not know who I am?"

The Marquis stopped dead, feeling as though the air was singing around his ears. In the same moment Selina came closer so that he could see her properly.

"Oh, Ian," she exclaimed. "Your face!"

"*Selina*?" he croaked in a low whisper. "Selina?"

"That's right and you didn't know me. Admit it now, you didn't."

"I thought I was going mad when your voice came out of nowhere. *Selina*!"

Relief, astonishment and admiration, all swept him.

The next moment he had swept her up into a giant hug, laughing as he did so.

Selina clasped him back, giggling in triumph.

"You wretch! What a start you gave me!"

"But I fooled you, didn't I?"

He gave her a little shake.

"Yes, you did." he admitted, looking down into her face. "I ought to wring your neck."

He pulled her close again, hugging her tightly. For a moment Selina let herself nestle against him, enjoying the warmth and enthusiasm of his embrace. It was so good to be in his arms – so safe and so comforting.

But then she felt him stiffen and push her gently away from him.

"Yes," he carried on and his voice sounded rather awkward. "Yes, well – you're here now. You should have been back sooner. I was concerned."

"It's not easy to buy clothes, you know."

"Let me look at you."

He stood back to gain a better view and a quizzical, slightly shocked expression came over his face.

"*My dear girl!*"

"What's wrong?" she asked defensively.

"You are supposed to be my valet. No valet ever looked like that, not if he wanted to keep his job."

He peered at her more closely.

"And just what are you wearing under your coat?" he demanded suspiciously.

Proudly she opened her coat wide to display the full glory of the waistcoat. The Marquis stared at it, stupefied, for a whole minute.

"What on earth do you call that thing?" he asked at last in a dazed voice.

"It's a waistcoat."

"Indeed?"

"Yes, indeed."

"Well, let me tell you this, my dear girl, among the hoipolloi it might well be known as a waistcoat, but among gentlemen of fashion it would be called pig fodder!"

"You are very rude," she exclaimed indignantly.

"Not as rude as I feel. Am I seriously supposed to go out in your company with you wearing that object?"

"*I* think it's very smart."

"So I would have supposed. Why, it's – it's just – I don't know how to describe it."

He covered his eyes in anguish.

Selina looked down at her waistcoat.

"I thought it very colourful – "

"Oh, yes," he concurred faintly. "It's colourful."

She explained about the young man who had not come to pay for his clothes.

"He must have gambled the money away."

"How can you possibly know that?"

"Because that particular waistcoat could only have been chosen by a man with more money than sense."

"*I* chose it."

"*You*, Selina, are not a man," he growled through gritted teeth, leaving the implication hanging in the air.

Then he sighed.

"Oh well, it can't be helped."

"It's not really so bad, is it, Ian?"

"Yes, it really is just that bad. If you must wear the thing, button up your coat and try to look as though we're not together."

Selina chuckled.

"All right, I'll keep my distance and not embarrass you. But I didn't really do so badly, did I?"

As she was speaking she tapped the top hat which, incredibly, had stayed in place during their vigorous hug.

The Marquis stared.

"Take it off at once," he ordered sharply.

She removed the top hat with a flourish, giving him a good view of her carefully arranged locks and made him an elegant little bow.

"Oh, Selina, no!" he breathed.

Startled by his horrified look, she enquired,

"Whatever is the matter?"

"Your hair! Your beautiful hair! How could you cut it all off?"

"But – "

"There was no need for that. You could have piled it up somehow – "

"Not convincingly, that's why I – "

"But you didn't have to go to such lengths. It was *so* lovely."

Selina smiled at him.

"It can be lovely again."

"Yes, when it's grown, but that will take years."

"No. Just a few seconds, actually."

She pulled off the wig and her lovely long golden hair, which had been crammed beneath it, came loose and cascaded over her shoulders.

She heard a sharp intake of his breath and saw the blinding delight that came over his face.

"You – " he grimaced, "you – "

86

She waited for what he would say next, feeling sure that his words would be as wonderful as the heartfelt joy in his eyes.

But she was never to know.

Before he could say a word they heard the sound of the landlord humming loudly as he returned with wine and the Marquis seemed to freeze.

"You had better get out of sight," he urged. "We'll be leaving almost at once."

Selina nodded and hurried away upstairs. It was disappointing, but she told herself she had gained a small victory.

The response she had seen in his eyes, the caressing way he had muttered, "your beautiful hair," meant that she could hope for better things. She had only to be patient.

In her room she hastily braided her hair and fitted it more securely beneath her wig.

She said her goodbyes to Martha and Simpkins and noted with amusement that they were arguing again.

Below Lovall and Wilkins were loading the last of the bags onto the wagons. Wilkins would take the chaise to Castleton Hall, whilst Lovall would follow Selina and the Marquis to Portsmouth.

The Marquis was already in the seat of the curricle. Selina looked up, expecting him to offer his hand to help her aboard, but he merely looked at her, grinning.

"Hurry up, boy. Don't keep me waiting."

"Oh yes, I forgot."

She hopped nimbly up and he swung his horses out of the yard.

"A man does not help another man into his chaise," he lectured her as they sped out of the town. "Especially when that other man is supposed to be his valet."

"Then you had better instruct me in my duties, sir."

"There's nothing for you to learn, except that you must remember you are no longer a lady."

"But aren't I supposed to look after your things and advise you what to wear?"

The Marquis visibly winced.

"If you imagine that I am going to ask advice from someone capable of buying that dreadful monstrosity that is still, unfortunately, visible beneath your coat, then you have windmills in your head!"

"Oh dear, and I was going to offer to tell you where you can buy one like it."

This time he just gave her a look.

After they had bowled along cheerfully for a few miles, he reflected,

"I've been thinking that you cannot possibly pass as my valet."

"I'll take the waistcoat off," she offered unselfishly.

"Thank you. I do appreciate your generosity. But, even without it, I fear you wouldn't strike the right note of workaday decorum. Plainly you're a devilish young blade, up to every lark – out on a spree."

"Then who are *you*?"

"I am your uncle, coming along to keep an eye on you. You dear mother begged me with tears in her eyes to protect her darling Cedric from the big bad world!"

"*Cedric*?" she echoed in disgust. "You don't really expect me to be called Cedric, do you?"

"It's a perfectly good name."

"It most certainly is not. When I was a child we were visited by one of my Papa's cousins, who brought her eight year old son, called Cedric."

"Did he bully you?"

"No, according to his mother it was the other way round. He simply had no spirit. He couldn't climb trees or hunt for frogs' spawn, fly a kite or do anything of interest."

"And you could do all these things?"

"Of course. Papa taught me."

"How old were you at the time?"

"Six."

"And eight year old Cedric didn't impress you?"

"I feel quite certain," she said firmly, "that nobody called Cedric could possibly be a devilish young blade. He is more likely to cry for his Mama when his feet get wet."

The Marquis laughed.

"Is that what he did? Then I can only apologise, because I've quite decided that your name is to be Cedric. And no pleas or arguments will move me."

"You're just wreaking revenge for my waistcoat!"

"Well, revenge is very sweet."

"All right, I shall become the Honourable Cedric Ponsonby – out on a spree."

"Good. And I'll address you as Ponsonby."

"That's better than Cedric. What shall I call you?"

"Castleton."

"I cannot do that," she exclaimed, scandalised.

"It's just what you would do if you really were the Honourable Cedric Ponsonby."

Selina tried to assume the right manner.

"I say, Castleton old boy," she barked in a neighing voice, "what time shall we get to this place we're heading for, eh? What? What?"

"Don't overdo it," he cautioned repressively.

"I am going to enjoy this!"

"That's what I'm afraid of. By the way, where did you find that aggressive character you assumed in the tap room? I've met men like him, but surely you haven't?"

"Several of my stepfather's friends are exactly like him."

"I can now see why you didn't want to marry any of them."

The horrible thought reminded her of just why they were making this journey and for a moment a cloud hung over her.

"Don't worry," assured the Marquis, showing the quick understanding she was beginning to find so loveable. "I will not allow anything to happen to you."

They changed horses twice and pressed on as far as possible. It was eight o'clock in the evening before they pulled into *The Three Acorns* post house.

"I hope we will be able to find rooms," the Marquis sounded worried. "It looks rather crowded."

It seemed a comfortable inn, although rather small. The Marquis entered with his winning smile and asked if they had rooms available for himself and his young friend, as well as somewhere for his groom.

The landlord replied civilly that his inn was almost full, but he could just manage to squeeze them in.

"One room is ready now, my Lord, and the second one will be available in an hour. The gentleman who has been occupying it is just leaving."

"Ponsonby, you take the one that's available now," suggested the Marquis. "And the other will be available when we've had dinner, I daresay."

Lovall brought in their bags and took them upstairs.

Selina's room proved plain and rustic but spotlessly clean. There were two small beds with patchwork quilts, a dresser and a wardrobe made of oak. The Marquis came to inspect it and direct Lovall to leave the bags there.

"Serviceable for one night," was his verdict. "But I would not like to be here longer. It's rather noisy. Some of the men in the tap room are getting rowdy."

"Perhaps we ought to join them," Selina proposed mischievously. "You can introduce me to the mysteries of strong drink."

"I am supposed to be protecting you from the worst excesses!"

"But surely strong drink cannot be one of the worst excesses?" she argued, eyes glinting. "I am sure there are far worse and  – "

"Well, you're not going to discover them with me," he replied desperately. "Selina, are you trying to drive me grey-haired?"

"No, but Ponsonby is," she reminded him.

"I mean, of course, Ponsonby."

"He's such a terrific daredevil is young Ponsonby," she countered, getting into her stride. "After dinner I think he would like to go out on the town  – "

"After dinner he is going to do as he is told and go to bed," the Marquis stipulated firmly. "After all, I did promise his mother  – "

There was a knock on the door.

Selina opened it to find a voluptuously built young woman wearing a very low cut dress that left no doubt of her charms. In her hands she carried two tankards.

"If you please, sir," she said, looking languishingly at 'Ponsonby', "the landlord sent you some of our best ale, compliments of the house."

Selina cleared her throat and declared,

"That's very kind of him."

"Shall I bring them into your room, sir?" she asked softly.

"Er – yes, thank you my – my dear."

The maid came in and laid the tankards down. She offered a polite smile to the Marquis, but the full blaze of her eyes was reserved for his young friend.

"My name is Betty, sir. Can I do anything more for you?"

"I don't think so," Selina answered briefly.

"It's no trouble, sir. Anything at all?"

The Marquis was observing this scene with unholy glee, but at this point he felt impelled to intervene.

"That will be all, thank you so much," he insisted, proffering a coin, the size of which made Betty's eyes pop. In a moment he received all her attention and he took the chance to remove her from the room.

"Ian," asked Selina, aghast, "did she mean what I thought – ?"

"She meant just that," he laughed, "You made quite a conquest. At least, you did until I cut you out. It's the power of money, I am afraid. You are a fine upstanding young gentleman, but *I* had the gold."

"Goodness gracious!"

"The sooner we dine and retire the better."

The food was excellent.

They were served by Betty who, despite the power of the Marquis's money could not stop herself sighing over the handsome young gentleman.

The Marquis treated her with the exquisite courtesy he always showed even to the lowliest servants.

Selina wondered if he admired Betty. Perhaps he liked buxom women.

She considered her own figure with some dismay. Without being exactly flat-chested she knew she could not compete with Betty. And she had big feet, which he would certainly know about now, she thought gloomily.

Over the beef the Marquis began to talk about his house and his plans for it.

"It has taken me some time to consider it my own," he began. "I grew up thinking of it as Jack's birthright and for a long time I felt like an impostor.

"But when I return from this trip I have plans, not just for the house but also for the village. For one thing, there is a derelict building by the Church, which I own, and which I mean to turn into a village hall with proper seating for an audience."

"What would you need it for?" Selina asked.

"For one reason, there is not a decent place in the village where they can meet at Christmas. And then there are travelling shows and my people miss out because there is nowhere for them to perform."

Selina nodded, noting the unconscious 'my people'. It somehow pleased her that the Marquis felt like a father to those who depended on him.

"And it will be a suitable place for meetings when speakers come to talk to them about politics."

"Politics?" She sounded a bit startled. "But what's the point when they have no vote?"

"But they will have one day. The world changes."

"But how can they use a vote when they have no education?"

"I must see to it that they do receive an education."

Selina had never before heard ideas like these.

Her parents had been very kindly people, but they had accepted without question that there was a hierarchy in which most people were their social inferiors.

But the Marquis looked beyond his own interests, asking himself how he could benefit others.

Suddenly she felt exhilarated.

In a mysterious way the world was a better place because he was a good man.

"It's lucky that I am dressed like this tonight," she exclaimed.

"Why?"

"Because you are discussing serious ideas with me, 'man to man'. If I looked like a woman, you wouldn't."

"I suppose there's something in that, but I think – in fact I know – I would have wanted to talk seriously to you in any case. I want to tell you all about my home and everything I am trying to achieve, because I think you are the one person who could understand – "

He broke off as he saw the landlord hovering.

"My Lord," he said nervously, "a terrible thing has happened. I'm afraid I cannot let you have the other room. The man supposed to be leaving it is drunk and refusing to go. He has barricaded the door and I am unable to get in.

"Please forgive me, but I am afraid you and your friend will have to sleep in the same room."

# CHAPTER SEVEN

For a moment Selina did not register the meaning of the words. It simply was not possible that the landlord had just said what he had said.

She swallowed nervily and looked at the Marquis. But far from being in any way concerned, he displayed a cool indifference.

"Surely some way could be found of opening the door?" he asked the landlord languidly.

"My Lord, we have tried charging it, but he seems to have wedged a large item of furniture behind it and the door cannot be shifted."

The Marquis yawned elaborately.

"Well then, it's a devilish unsatisfactory business. I shall simply have to take over your room, landlord."

"You could do so, my Lord, with my good will, but my wife is a very determined woman and she says that if anyone tries to enter, she will use the poker on them!"

"My dear fellow, I shouldn't like to put the lady to the trouble of using the poker. Let me see if my powers of persuasion can work on your disobliging guest."

They followed the landlord up the stairs, falling a little way behind in order to have a muttered conversation.

"Ian, what are we going to do?"

"Say nothing, do nothing. Don't let anyone see that you are disconcerted. That would attract attention, which we must on no account do."

She recognised the force of this argument and fell silent, but she was full of dread.

They arrived at the room that should have been the Marquis's and found a little crowd of maids and potboys, all eager to enjoy the excitement.

Selina tried not to meet Betty's eye.

It soon became apparent that the Marquis's powers of persuasion were not going to be up to this challenge, as his opponent was drunk to the point of imbecility.

A one-sided conversation ensued with the Marquis offering the drunk a handsome sum to vacate the room and was rewarded by a sea shanty, sung out of tune.

Then he increased the offer and something smashed on the other side of the door hard enough to make it shake.

"I seem to be having little success," he concluded with a sigh.

"You can 'ave my room" one of the potboys piped up, adding, "for the same money you offered 'im."

"Hush your mouth," the landlord roared. "Take no notice of him, my Lord. He sleeps over the stables with three others. You wouldn't like it."

"No, I do believe I wouldn't," admitted the Marquis with a grim shudder. "No matter. There are two beds in Ponsonby's room. You won't mind me having the other one, will you old fellow?"

His hand was tight on Selina's shoulder, urging her to follow his lead. She smiled and replied gruffly.

"Not at all, Castleton. Glad to help."

The Marquis thumped her on the back.

"Good man! And now that that's settled, I suggest we return below and finish our meal. Landlord, how good is your best brandy?"

"As good as you'd expect so near to the coast, my Lord," answered the landlord with a wink.

"Then I'll have a glass."

"And so will I," piped up 'Ponsonby' with a defiant glance at his 'uncle', who maintained a diplomatic silence.

When they were seated, Selina muttered urgently,

"Ian, whatever are you thinking about?"

"Well, you clearly think that I am going to forget my promise to behave exactly like a gentleman and force my attentions on you."

"I didn't – I never – "

She was blushing furiously.

"You goose," he told her lightly. "I shall have to go in there with you, but when the inn is quiet, I shall leave unobserved and go outside."

"Outside where?"

"Anywhere. It's a fine night. I can sleep under the stars."

"But you can't do that."

"I must. I cannot stay inside the building. There's too much chance of my being seen. We're both safer if I sleep outside."

"But won't you be seen outside?"

"There's a little copse of trees to hide me. And it's summer. I won't catch cold."

"How kind you are," she cried impulsively. "I feel dreadful making you do such a thing."

"It isn't you that makes me," he pointed out, "but our inebriated friend. This is only for one night and then, tomorrow, we'll go and leave all the problems behind us."

The brandy then arrived and the landlord set a glass before each of them and retired.

Selina watched as the Marquis picked up the full bellied glass, cradled it in his palm and inhaled the aroma before taking a sip.

"Now you," he ordered.

Carefully following his lead, she swirled the liquid around the bowl, attempting to look as though this came naturally to her and then sipped.

At once she gagged. Nothing had prepared her for the fiery liquid.

The Marquis thumped her on the back.

"That's no way to treat good brandy."

"Why didn't you warn me?" she asked hoarsely.

"Because you wouldn't have believed me. Besides, I thought you wanted to experiment with a life of excess."

"The joys of excess are greatly exaggerated. You can tell Mrs. Ponsonby that her little Cedric is going to be abstemious from this moment on."

"She'll be delighted to hear it," he laughed.

He tipped her brandy into his own and sipped it, his eyes laughing at her over the rim of the glass.

"What did the landlord mean about being near the coast?" enquired Selina.

"It was his way of hinting that the liquor is brought in unofficially, by 'the gentlemen'."

"You mean smugglers?"

"Yes I do."

"What fun! Tell me all about it."

"You are reacting improperly," he reproved her. "Anybody would think you were delighted at encountering this criminal activity. A female of delicacy should swoon with shock."

Selina's lips twitched.

It was getting late and the lights were going out as they climbed the stairs together.

Selina, trying to look as though she did not have a care in the world, opened the bedroom door and walked in, followed by the Marquis.

She could not help feeling intensely self-conscious.

It seemed that every second she grew more strongly attracted to the Marquis and this sudden enforced intimacy was almost overwhelming.

She was swept by the strength of her own feelings, and turned away to the window, hoping he would not see her blush.

"That's it," he said, following her to the window and pointing to a patch of green behind the inn. "That little clump of trees over there. I'll be nice and cosy."

Selina now recovered her composure.

"Speaking as your valet, my Lord, I should advise you to wear your least elegant clothes lest the ground ruin them."

"Good grief, Ponsonby! You don't seriously think I am travelling with anything suitable for sleeping on the ground? What a lot you must learn before you can become a man of fashion! After tonight I shall discard them."

"Take something warm to wrap in, then."

"A very good thought." He took a cloak from the wardrobe. "This will do. Of course, one should be willing to sacrifice mere clothes – "

He added wickedly,

"Can I borrow your waistcoat?"

"Certainly not. Goodnight, my Lord."

The Marquis crept out into the corridor and stood listening for any sound from the darkened building. From the tap room came the hum of a few late revellers.

He slipped outside without being seen and walked away from the inn, heading across the patch of grass.

Selina, standing at the window, watched him go till he vanished among the trees.

She was thoughtful as she took off her clothes and climbed into bed.

Who would have believed that so many incredible things could have happened in such a short time? It was only three days since she had fled her stepfather's house, yet it seemed like a lifetime.

Selina had met the Marquis and already she could not imagine the world without him.

He was amazingly unlike the dashing lover she had imagined might carry her off.

For one thing, he was a bit older than the man in her romantic dreams, but his sweet temper, his quiet charm and perfect kindly courtesy had enchanted her, as the brash manners of younger men never did and he had now come to mean everything to her.

What did she mean to him? she wondered.

Nothing probably.

He regarded her as a child that he was humouring.

How very quick he had been to assure her that his behaviour would be entirely proper! Of course, she would not wish it any other way, she assured herself.

But it was sad that he seemed to find the promise so easy to keep.

After all, would one little improper advance be so terrible?

Instantly she caught herself up in horror. It was a shocking thought and one that no truly refined lady would have entertained for a moment.

With a sigh she decided that she must be lacking in the right delicate instincts. And no doubt he thought so too and disapproved of her.

On that depressing thought she snuggled down and went to sleep.

*

She was woken by a loud clap of thunder.

After a while she realised that the pounding noise she could hear was rain, pouring down and hammering on the roof. It must be one of the summer storms that seemed to occur in even the finest weather.

Suddenly she sat up in bed.

*The Marquis*!

He was caught out there in this weather. He must be drenched. He might catch pneumonia.

She rushed to the window and looked out into the darkness, but there was no sign of him. He was probably huddled under the inadequate shelter of a tree.

Surely he would be sensible and find some cover, even if it was only a barn?

But in her heart she knew that he would not return unless she fetched him herself. He would regard anything else as a violation of his word.

Throwing off her nightdress, she began to pull on her breeches and shirt. When she had put on her boots and drawn a cloak about her shoulders she was ready to leave.

Her heart in her mouth, she crept down through the dark building and out through the back door.

The wind hit her like a blow and made her stagger back against the wall.

But she recovered and then forced herself to press on, lashed by rain towards the small clump of trees, which she could just make out against the sky.

When she was there she began to call his name.

"Ian! *Ian*!"

There was no reply and she began to be afraid that he had already hurried away, making her efforts useless.

"*Ian*!"

The wind threw her voice back at her.

"Ian – please – can you hear me?"

"Selina – what the devil are you doing here?"

To her overwhelming relief she could make out his voice coming from within the trees. She pushed forward and saw him emerging from some bushes.

"Selina! What possessed you to come here?"

"I came to fetch you. You cannot stay out in this."

"But I must – "

"I will not take no for your answer," she cried out desperately. "You cannot stay out here and catch cold."

He stood undecided, rain pouring onto his head and down his face.

At last he muttered,

"It is very sweet of you, but I don't really think – "

She stamped her foot in the mud.

"If you won't think of yourself, think of *me*," she shouted over the wind. "If anything happens to you, what would I do?"

"I suppose you are right."

"I am not going back without you. We'll just have to be very careful."

"In that case," he urged her gratefully, "let's hurry."

The heavy rain had turned the ground to quagmire, and they had to cling together to stop themselves sliding about as they made their way back to the inn.

As they approached, Selina knew a moment's fear, lest anyone had found the door unlocked and had locked it behind her.

But their luck held and in a few moments they were upstairs in the room with nobody having seen them.

At first they just clung together, shivering.

"Bless you!" he murmured at last. "I don't know what I would have done without you. I was not expecting a storm."

"Put some dry clothes on," she ordered him briskly. "Where can I find something?"

"That case," he pointed. "I have a dressing gown."

For the moment her self-consciousness had waned, replaced by a strong desire to look after him. She found a dressing gown with a thick white towel embroidered with the Castleton monogram. She handed it to him and he put it over his head, rubbing vigorously.

She found another towel for herself.

She had not put on her wig to go outside and now her long hair was streaming with water. She threw aside her coat and dried herself as best she could.

"Selina, I – "

She turned to find the Marquis staring at her with a thunderstruck look on his face.

In that moment she became aware that without her coat there was nothing to disguise the immodest way the breeches clung to her and outlined her figure. She blushed and lowered the towel so that it partially covered her.

But then she noticed something about him that took her mind off herself.

He had removed his coat and was standing in his shirt and breeches, both of them soaking. As she watched he reached for his dressing gown and started to pull it on.

"No," she called out firmly.

He looked startled.

"Perhaps it's time I started acting as your valet after all. A good valet would insist that you not to put on your dressing gown till you have replaced your wet clothes with dry ones."

"But my dear, how can I?"

"The same way I can. We could both catch chills if we don't change completely."

"You are right. Your generous action in rescuing me would be wasted if it is left incomplete. Half measures will not do."

"We shall just have to be strong-minded about it."

"I agree."

"Yes."

"Yes."

She hoped he could not see her blushing. And yet, it did not seem very terrible when he was so kind.

Turning her back on him and moving very fast, she managed to climb back into her nightdress and pull out a shawl from her bag.

When she looked round he, too, had removed all of his wet clothes and was wearing the brocade dressing gown over what appeared to be a nightshirt.

"I do hope my bare feet don't offend you," he said apologetically.

"No, you must make sure to dry them properly too. My Mama always said that damp feet are dangerous."

He smiled and suddenly it did not seem alarming, but rather cosy and domestic.

She gave a sudden chuckle.

"What is it?" he asked.

"I was thinking what a pickle we would have been in if I had been travelling as a woman."

"My goodness, yes!"

"I think we were brilliant to have had the idea."

*"We* were brilliant?"

"Yes, to think of me being a boy."

"That was your idea, Selina."

"Surely, it was yours, too? When we talked, were you not just about to suggest the same deception?"

He gave her a strange smile.

"No, my idea was quite different."

"Better than this?"

She thought his smile grew a little wistful, though she could not imagine why.

"Much better," he muttered gently.

"What was it? Do tell me?"

But he shook his head.

"It doesn't matter for now. I thought – well, I was mistaken."

"But Ian – "

"Is all of this enough of an adventure for you?" he interrupted her, speaking lightly but determinedly.

"Enough to last for ever," she replied. "After this, I won't complain if the rest of my life is extremely dull."

"You say that now, but you're very young. You've time to change your mind and seek new excitement."

"I've already had much more excitement than most women ever know in their lifetime."

"But then you were born for it, Selina. Adventure is your natural atmosphere. You cope with the unexpected so well. Nothing can throw you off your stride. You dealt with the Duke, you solved Martha's problem, you came to my rescue in the storm. I cannot imagine anything that you could not face with aplomb."

'Except what I am beginning to feel for you,' she mused. 'I don't think I can cope with that very well.'

"Is something now the matter?" he asked, seeing a faraway look on her face. "Did I say anything wrong?"

"No, you are being very kind, much too kind. I am not really like that at all."

"I don't think you realise what you are truly like. Most of us don't till something extraordinary happens and then our real self emerges and next we discover we're quite different from what we thought."

"Yes," she murmured. "Something extraordinary happens and then nothing is ever the same again."

"Perhaps we should try to sleep now."

He climbed into the other bed and pulled the covers up around his shoulders.

Selina turned out the lamp and slid down into her bed, listening to the sound of his breathing.

She lay quiet and still, feeling sure that she would not sleep a wink.

Her mind was full of his words.

He had said that adventure was her natural life and it seemed at this very moment that nothing could be more wonderful than to travel on with him for ever seeking new horizons.

But he would probably find it dull, she thought. He was naturally a grave and serious man and although he had said that he enjoyed laughing in her company, she did not place too much reliance in his assertion.

To him this was probably like a holiday before he returned to the serious business of caring for his people.

And helping him would be nice too, she mused.

If only her stepfather did not appear and try to drag her back. The thought was even more terrible now that she had met the Marquis.

Surely he would defend her?

But her stepfather was very brutal and determined. How could anyone protect her from him – ?

*He seemed to be chasing her down a long corridor. She ran as fast as possible, but it was of no use. He was gaining on her.*

*She screamed for the Marquis to save her, but she knew he could not hear. He had abandoned her and she would never see him again. Then she screamed again – in misery and desolation.*

"Selina – *Selina* – "

"Let me go," she cried, fighting the hands that held her. "Let me go, I won't go back – "

"Selina, it's me, Ian." The Marquis gave her a little shake. "Wake up."

With a gasp she awoke to find herself sitting up in bed. He was there with her, holding her arms and looking anxiously into her face.

"My dear girl, you were having a nightmare."

"I thought *he* had found me," she whispered, "and I was running and running away from my stepfather and it was no use because I can never get away from him – "

"Yes, you will," he soothed. "Trust me. I won't let him take you back."

"You couldn't stop him," she wept.

"Yes, I could. Selina, I promise you that I will do anything necessary, anything at all, to save you from him. Do you believe me?"

She nodded her head, trying to look as though his words gave her confidence, but she could not quite manage it and something in her woebegone face made him take her swiftly in his arms, cradling her head on his shoulder.

He held her tightly against him, rocking her back and forth as if she was a child, murmuring softly.

"It's all right, it's all right. I'll take care of you. Nobody can take you while I am here with you."

It was such bliss to be held in his arms, feeling so completely safe and cared for. If only she could stay like this for ever.

For a short moment she allowed herself to forget everything else and cling onto him, tightening her arms and closing her eyes.

She supposed that what they were now doing would appear scandalous, but she only sensed that this was where she really belonged – with a man who made her feel that the world was a good place.

She trusted him.

She increasingly loved him.

But she dreaded being a burden to him.

"I am all right, truly," she said in a wobbly voice. "You must think – I'm a real crybaby."

"No, I think you are very brave. You've kept your courage up through difficulties that would have destroyed a lesser woman."

"But everything you said about me is wrong," she sniffed, " – about adventure being my element, and – and facing troubles with aplomb. I'm just a fraud."

"I forbid you to talk like that," the Marquis insisted firmly. "I wouldn't allow anyone else to criticise you and I will not allow you to do so either."

She gave a watery chuckle.

"That's better, Selina, do you think you can now go back to sleep?"

"Yes, I am sure I can. Thank you, Ian. I am sorry to be such a nuisance."

"You're not a nuisance. I'm glad if you let me care for you a little."

She lay down and fell asleep almost as soon as her head hit the pillow. Her last conscious thought was that he was still holding her hand.

*

She awoke to find that it was now morning and the Marquis, fully dressed, was sitting on the edge of her bed.

"I am going downstairs now, Selina. Hurry up and join me and then we'll be away from here."

He left the room without waiting for her reply. His manner had been coolly friendly, containing no hint of the brief intimacy they had shared the night before.

It might never have happened.

After the storm the sun shone brilliantly. A hurried breakfast and they were on the road again, bowling along merrily, knowing that their destination was just a few short miles away.

"I feel rather guilty," confessed Selina.

"Why should you?"

"I keep thinking of that poor girl, Felicity. Here we are escaping, but she still has to cope with her father."

"Yes, I feel bad about her, too," he admitted. "I would like to help her, if I could. In fact, I may be doing the best thing for her by vanishing. Her father can hardly bully her into marrying me if I am not around."

"I can already smell sea breezes, Ian. How much further to Portsmouth?"

"About three miles. Then with luck we'll find the yacht all ready to cast off. We'll hurry aboard and head for far shores."

As he spoke he increased his speed and in no time at all it seemed they could see Portsmouth ahead of them. Half an hour later they had reached the town.

Because the Marquis had been several times before, he drove with no difficulty through crowded streets until he reached the road which led down to the harbour.

Selina looked about her, delighted and relieved.

As they neared the sea the road climbed a little until they could look down to where ships were anchored.

Selina drew in her breath at the beauty of the sight.

The Marquis slowed the horses so he could study the ships and see whether his yacht was where he expected it to be.

"There she is," he exclaimed. "I knew my Captain would not let us down. Absolutely splendid. We can now begin to feel easy."

But from behind them came a sudden cry of alarm.

"My Lord! *My Lord*!"

The Marquis turned to where Lovall was driving the wagon.

"What is it, Lovall?"

"Danger, my Lord. Look down there, to your left."

The Marquis looked down to a large building near the water with a flight of shallow steps outside the main entrance.

On the top step stood two men.

Selina and he froze at the same moment as they recognised the Duke of Wendover and John Gardner.

# CHAPTER EIGHT

Selina was too astonished and horrified to speak.

The Marquis instinctively urged the horses on and they galloped along the high road overlooking the port.

They sped on till they were concealed by the fence that cut off the port from the road. Then the Marquis drew in the horses calling to Lovall as he did so.

"Well done! Thank God you warned us. I never for one moment expected we would find anyone here."

"They obviously worked out exactly what we were – going to do," Selina sighed in a trembling voice.

"The difficulty now is how to get to *The Mermaid* without being seen."

Lovall got out of the wagon. Going to the fence he pulled a loose board aside so he could see directly into the harbour below them.

There were only a few ships in port. The Marquis's yacht was anchored by itself some distance from the ticket office where their ambushers were standing like sentinels.

Without a word, the Marquis handed over the reins to Selina. Then he got out of the curricle and went towards Lovall, who had by now enlarged the hole in the fence.

After looking through, he said, in an urgent voice,

"Listen, Lovall. You must make your way slowly and carefully to *The Mermaid*. Inform the Captain to bring the yacht as near as possible to where we are now and be ready to cast off the moment we are on board."

"Very good, my Lord."

Without further ado he forced his way through the hole in the fence and hurried off to the port. They saw him begin to run towards *The Mermaid*.

Frowning the Marquis went back to the curricle.

"However could they know we were here?" asked Selina.

"I suppose it was obvious that if I had run away, I would go to my yacht and you would come with me."

"But how on earth did the Duke get in touch with my stepfather?"

"Perhaps his servants gossiped with mine. And, after we told him who you were, he might have sought out Gardner on purpose. Then they joined forces."

"I thought we had been so clever," sighed Selina.

"We shall have to be even cleverer from now on. Otherwise we shall lose everything."

"Oh, please, no, that must *not* happen."

"I don't intend to let it happen. Somehow we have to board the yacht without being seen."

"But it's impossible. It is still some distance away from us. How can we walk all that way unnoticed?"

"It's lucky you are in male clothes. They are not expecting that. We'll know more when Lovall returns."

After a few minutes Lovall climbed back through the fence. He was accompanied by three men who, from their garb, were sailors.

"We came to help, my Lord," said one. "The more hands the better."

"Good fellow! Lovall, what did the Captain say?"

"He's moving *The Mermaid* as near as he can, my Lord. Then I've seen a way you can go on board without anyone seeing you.

"On the other side of this 'ere fence there's a lot of planks of wood. They're obviously waiting for workmen to arrive and carry them down to a ship. The Captain says the best way to hide is to shield yourself behind planks."

The Marquis gave a sigh of relief.

"Then that's what I'll do."

"My Lord," Lovall then added, "the Captain also told me that the other yacht you see over there belongs to the Duke of Wendover, who arrived late last night."

The Marquis thought that this made matters even worse. Plainly the Duke was not going to give up easily.

But he did not mention this to Selina, not wanting to add to her worries. Instead he smiled and suggested,

"Selina, I have an idea for you. I'll explain it in a moment. Lovall, an important job for you. Change clothes with me quickly. Luckily we are about the same size."

In a couple of moments he had pulled on Lovall's plain clothes and the driver was luxuriously attired in the Marquis's long greatcoat and elegant hat.

"You'll do from a distance," grinned the Marquis with satisfaction. "Get up into the curricle and drive down past the ticket office. Go close to them so that they can see the Castleton arms on the side, but keep your collar up to hide your face. They must think it's me."

"Right, my Lord," enthused Lovall.

"Keep them chasing you as long as you can. Try to lose them. That will keep them confused. If they stop you, threaten to have the law on them for molesting an innocent man going about his lawful business.

"Then take the curricle back home. You'll have to abandon the wagon. Now, off with you."

Selina joined him at the gap in the fence and they watched as Lovall drove the curricle down to the buildings by the harbour, looking uncannily like the Marquis.

As instructed he slowed when he came to the ticket office and drove close, while keeping his head averted.

To his glee the Marquis saw his enemies start into life at the sight of the coat of arms on the curricle.

They dashed towards him, but Lovall whipped up the horses and sped off into the distance.

"How will they follow him?" queried the Marquis. "Do they have a vehicle handy? No. They must find one."

"It's looks as though they are having an argument," came in Selina.

Fearful as she was, she was able to enjoy the sight of her hated stepfather and the Duke turning on each other. Each was shouting.

There was much running backwards and forwards and waving of arms and then they collided.

Finally they managed to hail a passing carter and scramble into his ramshackle cart with more shouting and pointing.

Money passed and the carter set off.

"Will he catch Lovall?" Selina asked anxiously.

"It seems unlikely. But that doesn't mean we can relax. They will know which yacht is mine and will turn back when Lovall is out of sight. So we must still hurry."

"What must I do?"

"Get into the wagon, wrap your cloak around you, and pull some of the bags over you until you're completely covered. Don't move until the wagon stops and they start taking the luggage out."

He turned to his sailors.

"Get the carriage as close as you can to the ship and hurry this 'gentleman' aboard and out of sight. Mark, you drive. Harry, you, Frank and I will be workmen shifting wood down to the quay. Now Selina – into the wagon!"

She climbed in and lay down on the floor. Then the Marquis and Mark piled the lighter bags on top of her.

"It's best if I cover your face with a cloak," he said. "It won't be for long. Will you be all right?"

"Of course I will, "Selina replied confidently. "I'll do anything as long as we can get away."

Despite all her brave words there was a note in her voice which told the Marquis how frightened she was. He laid his strong hands over hers and she clasped him back.

"Drive carefully, Mark, you are carrying a precious cargo."

The sailor nodded, jumped up into the driving seat and they began to move.

The next stage should be easy, the Marquis thought. With Gardner and the Duke out of sight it seemed needless for him to take precautions not to be seen.

But he refused to be complacent.

The Duke probably had his servants hanging about, who would recognise him and report to their Master that they had seen him board his yacht.

He hoped he would not be too easily recognisable in Lovall's clothes. The real danger lay in his hair, which was in an elegant style that no servant would have worn.

"Frank, let me have your scarf," he requested.

Frank promptly tore off his scarf and the Marquis tied the scarf over his locks and they were ready.

Each took up a large plank of wood and the three of them made their way laboriously down to the quay with the Marquis in the middle.

No journey had ever felt so long.

Now and then he managed to look around the side of the plank and he could just make out the wagon being driven onto the quay.

He wondered what it could be like for Selina, being jolted along in semi-darkness and in his mind he sent her a silent message of encouragement.

Selina felt every bump on the floor of the wagon, and could see nothing, but it did not matter as she was full of hope. Just a little longer now and she would be safe.

The wagon came to a halt.

She heard voices, felt luggage being moved from around her and then Mark leaned down and whispered,

"We're here, sir – ma'am."

He was answered by a muffled giggle.

"This is it. Chin up. Now you slide gradually out and look to your left. You'll see the gangway leading up to the deck of *The Mermaid*. There's no sign of those two gentlemen, but you go up that gangway as fast as you can."

She thanked him and moved cautiously till her feet were on the ground. There was the gangway and at the top of it was a serious looking man, who she guessed must be the Captain. He beckoned her and she hurried.

As she reached the yacht he extended a hand to pull her aboard.

"You must now go straight below," he said. "His Lordship's orders. Peter, here, will show you the way.

She followed him below, down some wooden steps, along a narrow corridor and then through a door.

She found herself in a well-appointed cabin, larger than she had expected to find on a yacht.

Looking out of the porthole, Selina was thrilled to see three men carrying planks hurrying along the quay.

At the last minute the planks were tossed into the wagon that had been left beside a high wall. Then the three men sprinted aboard.

They had done it, she thought triumphantly.

The next minute there was a knock on her door and she opened it to find the Marquis.

She was in the mood to throw her arms about him, but the serious look on his face stopped her.

"Are you all right in here?" he asked quickly.

"Yes, truly. But Ian, isn't it wonderful?"

"I hope it may be, but we must not rejoice too soon. There is still much to do. Stay hidden in here. Don't come on deck, whatever you do. We'll move out as quickly as we can."

"But surely the Duke and my stepfather have gone? They haven't returned, have they?"

"No, there hasn't been time enough for that. But I did see two men standing on the quay watching us and I recognised one of them as the Duke's valet. So when his Master returns, they'll follow us in Wendover's yacht. We must get as far ahead of them as we can."

He left and she guessed he was going to the bridge.

Suddenly the ship swayed beneath her.

They were on the move.

Because she felt almost exhausted by tension Selina sat down on the bed and then lay back against the pillows.

'*We have escaped*, we have escaped,' she rejoiced.

Yet she was afraid. It had been too easy. She knew that her stepfather was not the man to give up.

It seemed a long time before the Marquis returned.

When he opened the door, she asked eagerly,

"Tell me what has happened."

"The Captain has seen another ship on the horizon," he reported, "and it could be the Duke's."

Selina gave a cry of horror.

"Oh, no! Suppose they overtake us. Even if they don't, how will we ever find anywhere to go if they are just behind us?"

"I've been considering this myself. There's nothing to be gained by being frightened. *The Mermaid* is very fast and, although it will be unpleasant, the Captain and I have a plan that may work.

"We are heading across the Channel in the direction of Brest in France. Normally we might have stopped there, but the plan now is to push on through the Bay of Biscay."

"The Bay of Biscay?" she queried doubtfully. "It has a reputation for being very stormy."

"You can get a lot of rough weather. But we have a good start and I mean to sail even further ahead. If we leave them behind, we can call in at Gibraltar without their knowing. Then *The Mermaid* will just sail on and they can follow her as far as they like."

"Are you quite sure *The Mermaid* is quicker than the Duke's yacht?"

"It's quicker than any yacht I have seen so far," the Marquis replied. "Now I am going to get us a drink."

He left the cabin and by the time he returned with champagne, *The Mermaid* was moving at a great speed.

"We're winning!" he exclaimed. "I've just looked through the telescope again and there is no sign of them, which means we are pulling away. I think we should drink to our first victory."

He poured the champagne and they clinked glasses.

"Now, Ian, will you please show me which cabin is mine."

"You don't like this one? This is the Master Cabin and it is yours, but let me tell you something that should interest you. When I was designing this yacht, I thought it was wrong for a yacht to have only one large cabin or, to put it more plainly, one large bed."

"You mean you have two large cabins?"

"What I have designed is not so much large cabins, but beds big enough for two people. So I can be in comfort without feeling that my guests are cramped."

He paused before he continued proudly,

"So there are four double beds on my yacht in all. It means fewer cabins for our guests but more comfort."

"It is very clever of you to think of doing so, Ian, I've often thought it was wrong for one person to have all the comforts while others are squeezed into small cabins."

"So you see, if you prefer to stay in this cabin you won't be making me suffer."

"I must see the other cabins first."

"I think you'll like the one nearest to this, which is known as the pink bedroom and planned particularly for beautiful young ladies."

Because she was feeling curious she went with him and found the pink cabin, which had a double bed in it and was, she thought, extremely pretty.

"Oh, yes, I would like to sleep here," she suggested. "I will feel I am sleeping in a flower bed and what could be more romantic than that?"

"I'll have your bags brought in here, Selina, and in an hour I will collect you for dinner."

Selina unpacked, washed in some hot water brought to her by Peter and dressed in a pretty blue gown with a blue ribbon in her hair.

When the Marquis came to escort her, he was in his dinner jacket. He offered her his arm and together they made their way up to the deck.

In the Saloon she found a table laid for two.

The most elegant dining room in the most luxurious house in England could not have matched this table with its gleaming white napery, its shining crystal and the roses by her plate.

The sun was setting and a fresh breeze was getting up and there were specks of foam on the waves, but the weather was still pleasant.

Selina turned right round so that she could see the horizon in all directions. Wherever she looked there was nothing but sea and no sign of another ship.

"It's fine, we must have left them behind by now," remarked the Marquis.

"Yes, I was wondering, but it's not all I want to see. The sunset is so magnificent."

"It's always best at sea, there is nothing so beautiful as this, except perhaps returning home and seeing my own house again after a long absence."

The sun was huge, floating above a narrow bank of cloud and turning it to red and next yellow fire. As they watched it softened, became mauve and later grey.

When they turned back to the table they found that many candles had been lit.

"I thought we should mark our escape in style," the Marquis commented.

His chef was an expert who knew how to produce the most delicious dishes in the confines of a ship's galley.

The meal was delicious and the Marquis engaged her in serious conversation.

This time she had a suggestion of her own to make.

"We were talking about the railways. Wherever they go, prosperity will follow. Perhaps you can influence somebody to site a station in your locality. It could do a great deal for your people."

He looked startled.

"Of course it could. I have been so full of plans to help them, but I never thought of a station. That is just what I must do."

He looked at her curiously.

"How grateful they would be to you if they knew that it was you who had inspired me."

"But it is you will do all the hard work."

"It is work that's well worth doing and that is the most satisfying thing of all. Selina, tell me something – "

But he could go no further for at that moment the ship gave a lurch and his champagne spilled over his hand.

"I think we are headed for stormy waters. Time to go below and batten down the hatches. It's a pity, because it has been a most pleasant evening."

She thought it was a shame for everything to end so soon, but the ship was beginning to toss severely and she knew she would not like the next few hours.

"What you have to do," the Marquis told her, "is to retire to bed and sleep until the sunshine comes out in the morning and by that time we will be nearly at Gibraltar."

"I hope you are right," she answered with feeling.

He came with her as far as her cabin door, giving her his arm so she could steady herself against the rolling of the yacht.

"Are you frightened?" he enquired, concerned.

"Certainly not," she told him firmly. "I am going to have a good night's sleep."

"Well done."

But her smile faded as soon as she had closed the cabin door. She did manage to undress and climb into bed, hoping that the movement would not feel so bad when she was lying down.

She remembered the night that she and the Marquis had spent in the same room and wished he could be with her now.

'I expect being a man he will not be frightened and he won't mind the pitching and tossing however bad it may be,' she told herself.

At that moment the ship reared up so violently that she was tossed up from her bed and seemed to hang in the air for a moment before crashing down.

'Oh, help!' she screamed inwardly and buried her head under the pillow.

So muffled was the sound that she barely heard her cabin door open and someone come in.

"Selina?"

She emerged from her pillow to find the Marquis standing beside her bed.

"Forgive me for coming in, Selina, but I wanted to see how you are."

"Splendid, Ian, everything's wonderful."

"You're not scared?"

"Of course I am not scared. And why should I be? What is there to be scared of?

"*Whoa*!"

The cry came from her as the yacht heaved into the air. For a timeless moment it seemed to pause and then it plunged with a force that shook the Marquis off his feet.

He fell onto the bed landing on top of Selina.

For a moment she stared at him. Her face betrayed the fear she would not admit and his eyes were tender.

"Selina – "

He took her into his arms, meaning only to comfort her, but the next moment his lips were on hers and he was kissing her passionately.

Selina felt herself responding joyfully.

This was just what she had hoped and longed for.

Now it was happening everything inside her told her that it was right.

Strange excitements surged through her and she felt as though her whole body was turning into molten fire in his embrace.

He kissed her again and again and she clung to him, kissing him back and thrilled by the feel of his mouth, its urgency and its gentle persuasiveness.

Somewhere a million miles away a vast storm was raging on the ocean, but it was as nothing compared to the storm raging in her heart.

Beneath her, the ship heaved and lunged, but she was no longer afraid.

She was not afraid of anything in the world at this very moment.

"Selina," he whispered against her lips, "*Selina*."

Then his voice changed.

As if in a dream she heard him murmuring, "dear God, what am I doing?"

Suddenly she could feel the tossing of the ship.

It seemed as though hours had passed since she had been aware of anything but him and the feel of his lips on hers. In that delight all other sensations were blotted out.

But now delight was fading and dread was taking its place as he whispered terrible words.

"Selina – dear God, this is the last thing I meant to happen – after all I tried to – "

The horror on his face was obvious and it chilled her heart. Something that had been a glorious experience to her was an embarrassment to him.

"I never intended – Selina. It's unforgivable – "

"Ian – "

"I meant only to comfort you – I didn't want – you must believe me."

"I do believe you," she responded in a colourless voice. "Let's say no more."

"You are right. Promise me, Selina, you will forget that this ever happened and we can go on as before."

"I promise."

"That's very generous of you," he said awkwardly.

He got off the bed and went quickly to the door. It seemed to her that he could not escape quickly enough.

When he had gone, she lay staring miserably into the dark.

He did not love her. He had been briefly attracted – enough to kiss her, but he had fled before she became an 'entanglement'.

She could hear the screaming of the wind, but she was no longer scared.

'What did it matter?' she thought, as tears streamed down her face. 'What did anything matter beside the fact that he does not want me?'

\*

By morning the storm had blown itself out.

She was able to rise and dress steadily, wondering what the future could possibly hold now.

The Marquis came to take her to breakfast, smiling blandly as if nothing had happened the night before.

He was telling her that was how he wanted it, she

realised.  And she must appear to feel the same, if she was to keep her pride.

But her heart cried that she did not want pride.

She wanted love.

As they were walking along the narrow corridor she suddenly stopped.  They were standing outside one of the best cabins that he had shown her yesterday.

"What is it?" he asked.

"There are no other passengers, are there?"

"Of course not."

"I thought I heard a sound from behind that door."

"There shouldn't be anyone in there – "

But then the sound came again, a kind of scuffling.

Frowning, he opened the door and they walked in.

The cabin was empty.

And yet –

Selina sat on the bed and bounced up and down on it.  From underneath came a faint shriek.

She slid off and they bent down onto the floor.

The Marquis reached his arm under the bed.  There was the sound of scuffling again, a muffled squeal and he drew back, bringing something with him.

Something dusty and tousled that stared up at him – with a mixture of defiance and pleading.

The Marquis dropped his hands, aghast.

*"Felicity!"* he cried.

# CHAPTER NINE

Before their appalled eyes Lady Felicity Wendover brushed her clothes and looked at the Marquis sheepishly.

Then at Selina.

And then back at the Marquis.

Selina, looking at her closely in that split second, realised that, when the Marquis had described this girl as pretty, he had grossly understated the matter.

Lady Felicity was undoubtedly one of the loveliest young girls that Selina had ever seen. This was no mere pretty girl, but a great great beauty. Her violet eyes were huge and her mouth had a soft petulant droop calculated to make any man's head reel.

Her figure was voluptuous noted Selina with envy. Felicity could never have passed as a boy!

The Marquis could have married this real beauty.

And he did not want to.

*He did not want to*?

Suddenly that was very hard to believe.

Was he really running away from such a gorgeous creature? Would they now fall into each other's arms?

She held her breath.

"Hallo Ian," muttered Felicity. "*Surprise!*"

The Marquis did not look as though this surprise overwhelmed him with joy.

"Felicity, for pity's sake, what are you doing here?"

"I came because you were so caring," the girl told him anxiously. "I'll never forget how kind you were to me that evening. No one would even bother to listen to me, but you said you would help me. Don't you remember?"

"Of course I do, but – "

"And I had such a *terrible* quarrel with Papa. He said *terrible* things, and I said *terrible* things, and then he said more *terrible* things, and then I – "

"Yes, yes, you both said terrible things," added the Marquis hastily. "I understand that part."

"Do you? Do you really? I'm so glad because then you'll appreciate why I was forced to resort to desperate measures."

Her voice had a lisping though childlike quality that affected Selina like something squeaking across glass, but, to the male ear it might sound alluring and provocative.

"What desperate measures?" asked the Marquis.

"You ask me that?" she cried passionately.

"Yes, I did ask you," he said sounding anything but passionate.

"Isn't it obvious? *I've run away!*"

The Marquis covered his eyes.

Selina was beginning to feel better. He showed no signs of being distracted by love – distracted by irritation, more likely, she reckoned.

"How did you manage it?" he asked. "Didn't your father notice you were missing?"

"He'd already begun his journey with this horrible, vulgar man. He said you were pretending to be engaged to this man's daughter – or was it his stepdaughter? Well, it doesn't really matter, does it, because – ?"

"No, it doesn't matter," said the Marquis hurriedly.

"Anyway, this vulgar man – "

"My stepfather," volunteered Selina with a chuckle. "I'm Lady Selina Napier. How do you do."

"And how do you do," Felicity responded politely. "Oh, but it's all right then, isn't it? I mean, if you're going to marry Ian, *I* don't have to marry him."

"No," said Selina quickly. "That's just a story Ian cooked up for your father. We're not really engaged."

'And never will be,' she thought, remembering the hasty way he had ended their kisses, the embarrassment on his face and his desperation to avoid her.

"Oh dear," groaned Felicity. "That is such a pity. Are you sure you two couldn't get married? It would make everything so much easier."

Selina did not know whether to laugh or cry at this. Felicity's self-centeredness was so monumental that it had a humorous quality. You really could not be annoyed with someone so childlike.

Meeting the Marquis's eyes, she saw that he was thinking the same. It was disconcerting that their mental communication was so perfect at the very moment she was despairing of winning his love.

"Let's not go into that now," she said hastily. "You were saying about your father and my stepfather."

"Oh yes, it *was* stepfather, wasn't it? Of course it was, now I remember because he said his wife had been an Earl's daughter and thus his stepdaughter too was an Earl's daughter, so he, that is Papa, needn't think he was talking to a nobody, because he was related to two Earls through marriage and Papa said stuff and nonsense, only he put it more rudely than that, but I cannot repeat his exact words because I am a lady and the other man said – "

"Felicity," grated the Marquis through gritted teeth, "if you don't get to the point, I shall toss you overboard!"

Definitely not a lover, mused Selina.

"But I am coming to the point. It's difficult when you keep interrupting."

Seeing his fulminating eyes, she continued quickly,

"I heard them talking about how they were going to chase after you and that you'd probably go to Portsmouth because you had a yacht there.

"So I waited until they'd left and then I left too, to catch the mail coach. It's very fast, so I managed to reach Portsmouth before them. Then I just asked people until I found which ship was yours and I stowed away."

"But how the devil did you get on board?" growled the Marquis.

"There were men carrying supplies on board in big boxes. I managed to get into the warehouse and emptied one of the boxes. Then I got in. It was a tight squeeze, but not for long."

"And nobody noticed?" he demanded.

"Yes, one of your crewmen saw me, but I gave him a coin, so that was all right."

"Don't tell me who it was, I'd rather not know. So, you stowed away. Why?"

"Why – to throw myself on your mercy, of course."

"Felicity, I'm warning you, try to make sense."

"I need your help," she cried piteously. "You said you would help me. Didn't you mean it?"

"Of course I did, but in a general sense, but I didn't mean – oh, Heavens! What a mess!"

Without a warning Felicity burst into violent sobs. She sat down on the bed, her face buried in her hands and wept noisily.

For all his beautiful manners, the Marquis was no

better at dealing with this kind of situation than any other man.

"Felicity," he stammered, "please – I do beg you."

"I don't know who to turn to," she sobbed. "I'm desperate and you won't help me. Oh, what shall I *dooo*?"

The last word came out as a prolonged wail that had the desired effect of pushing the Marquis into sitting down beside her and make frantic efforts to comfort her.

"Now, come along, my dear girl. I'll help you, of course I will, but *do* be quiet."

"You will help me find Pierre, you really will?"

"Certainly – anything."

Felicity promptly threw her arms around his neck and sobbed even louder.

"Oh, thank you, *thank you*!"

Selina observed this fine performance with cynical interest. Clearly Felicity had brought the art of getting her own way to the point of genius.

"But where would you expect to find Pierre?"

"In Le Havre," Felicity spluttered. "He is waiting for me there until the fifteenth of this month. If I'm not there by then, he will know that *all hope is gone*."

"What will he do when all hope is gone?" Selina wanted to know.

"Join the French Navy," replied Felicity tragically. "There's a Recruiting Office in Le Havre. But we will get there in time, won't we?"

"I shouldn't think so," said the Marquis, alarmed.

"But of course we will. It must be hours since we left Portsmouth and Le Havre is the nearest French port. Pierre chose it because his parents live there and he knew I would have to come through Portsmouth."

"But we are not going to Le Havre. We are headed for Gibraltar. We have just crossed the Bay of Biscay."

Felicity gave a shriek and burst into sobs again.

This was now as much as the Marquis could stand. Indicating that Selina should sit on Felicity's other side, he pushed the howling girl towards her and made for the door.

"Try to shut her up before she rouses the crew – "

"But where are you going?"

"I'm going to tell the Captain to turn back. We are going to have to reach Le Havre by the fifteenth or die in the attempt!"

"But suppose we encounter the Duke's boat? What will you do?"

"*Sink it.*"

When he had departed, Selina found that she and Felicity were soon on better terms than might have been expected. Without a man to appreciate her performance, Felicity abandoned it with comical promptness and began to talk like a moderately sensible female.

"Will he really get me back to Pierre in time?" she asked Selina.

"I am sure he'll strain every nerve."

In a few minutes they felt the boat slow and begin a wide turn.

The Marquis then returned, bearing food.

"You must be feeling hungry," he said to Felicity. "Have you been under the bed all this time?"

She nodded.

"I got underneath when the yacht began to toss so violently. It felt safer. Are we now turning back?"

"Yes. Luckily the storm has blown itself out so the way back should be easier than the crossing. And we are going closer to the shore, because your father is following us, so that way we will avoid him."

Selina half expected Felicity to become upset at the knowledge that her father was in pursuit, but she showed no reaction. Evidently now that a man had taken charge, she considered everything settled.

The Marquis spoke quietly to Selina.

"A word with you, if you would be so kind."

They left Felicity munching happily and moved out onto the deck. Now that the storm had abated the morning air was pleasant.

"In one sense this makes things more difficult," he reflected, leaning on the rail and looking out to sea. "But in another sense it might be the perfect answer."

"You are going to help reunite her with Pierre?"

"I cannot see any other choice. If she is desperate enough to do this, then her wishes should be respected."

"And she did it all on her own?" mused Selina. "I thought I was daring, but I had you to help me."

"She's certainly displayed more spirit than I would have credited her with," he agreed. "And I'm not going to thwart her. We'll do our best to find Pierre and help them marry. Then let Wendover do his worst."

"And what will you do when we're safe from him?" Selina enquired.

She thought he hesitated before replying quietly,

"That depends on you."

Which was an answer you could take in so many different ways.

*

Their luck held. By hugging the shore they avoided the Duke's boat for a long time. When it finally came into view, there was plenty of distance between them.

"Is that really him?" asked Selina, looking through the telescope the Marquis had handed her.

"Do you think he can see us?"

"If we can see him, he can see us. He'll turn back to follow us, but we are about to sail around Brest, so he'll lose sight of us very soon. By the time he does reach Brest we'll be hidden by land again. With good luck, we'll have landed at Le Havre while he is still wondering where we are."

"Will we make Le Havre by the fifteenth?"

"If this good weather continues, yes. But then we have to find Pierre. And we will, I swear that we will!"

The grim way he said this made her look at him.

"You really mean it, don't you?"

"Mean it? Of course I do. Because if we don't find him the prospect facing me is too ghastly. Do you realise, Selina, I might end up married to that – that – ? I mean, she's a nice girl, but have you listened to – *have you*?"

"Yes," she agreed, feeling light of heart again.

"Can you imagine wanting to be married to her? I mean – good grief! It doesn't bear thinking of!"

"It doesn't, does it?"

They stood side by side watching the coast slide by.

*

They reached Le Havre the following morning, the fifteenth. Selina took an immediate liking to the busy port where so many activities flourished. Here were trade and shipbuilding as well as the French Navy.

"We have to hurry," urged Felicity earnestly. "It's the fifteenth today."

"But if you know his parents' address we should be there in time," the Marquis pointed out.

The family lived close to the shore and, as Felicity for all her fluffy-headed ways had managed to memorise the address, they found it without trouble.

They found the house in uproar. Monsieur Ducros was tearing his hair, Madame Ducros was in tears.

It soon became apparent why.

Pierre had already left for the Recruiting Office.

"All because of that heartless girl who abandoned him," Pierre's mother sobbed.

"But I am that heartless girl," cried Felicity. "And I haven't abandoned him."

"Where is this Office, quickly," asked the Marquis in an urgent voice.

They obtained the address and then all piled into a carriage and headed off for the Recruiting Office.

"Oh, we mustn't be too late," wailed Felicity. "We simply mustn't."

"I could never agree more," added the Marquis with feeling.

He was sitting beside Selina and somehow his hand found hers gripping it tightly in his. She clasped him back, wondering if he even knew what he was doing.

At last the Office came into view. Hurrying inside, they saw a line of young men moving slowly towards an Officer at a desk, who was writing details down. As they watched in horror, Pierre reached the head of the line.

He was giving in his name and the Officer was now writing it down.

"Pierre!" screamed Felicity.

He looked up, saw her and began to move.

But the Officer at the desk was pointing out that he had already given his name.

The process had started.

"It's too late," shrieked Felicity.

"Oh, no, it isn't," shouted out the Marquis grimly. "Rescue party – *charge*!"

As one person they launched themselves forwards, seizing Pierre and bearing him bodily out of the Office to the waiting vehicle.

"*Move!*" called the Marquis to the driver. "As fast as you can."

Next they were well on their way, rattling along the street. As they rounded the corner Selina looked back and saw the Recruiting Officer on the pavement, shouting and waving his arms.

Pierre had the athletic body of a dancer and seemed to be a good-looking young man, although it was hard to be sure as he was hidden in Felicity's embrace.

Selina watched them, smiling with much pleasure at seeing lovers reunited. There was no doubt that these two belonged together.

She looked at the Marquis and saw that he too was grinning.

Then he turned his gaze onto her and something in his eyes threw her into confusion.

\*

At the Ducros house all was delight and rejoicing.

Father Barnard from the small Church in the next street had called in to ask the family if there was any news.

"I warned the Father that there would be a wedding about now," trumpeted Pierre, "although I couldn't tell him the exact date. But I did say it would be the fifteenth at the latest. So now we can go ahead and be married today!"

"Of course, of course," agreed the genial Priest. "If I may see the lady's papers?"

Felicity produced her passport, which he examined and pronounced satisfactory.

"And now yours?" he turned to Pierre.

Pierre felt in his pocket and his expression changed to one of horror.

"I took it with me to the Recruiting Office. It must have fallen out when you rescued me."

"I'm afraid that I cannot marry you without it," said Father Barnard apologetically.

"But Father, you know me," roared Pierre. "You baptised me."

"Indeed. But everything must be done in the proper way. I'm afraid that, without papers, I cannot marry you."

"What do I do?" asked Pierre, aghast. "I cannot go back there."

Felicity burst into sobs at this last-minute disaster. Selina too felt very much like crying.

After all they had just been through! How could this happen on top of everything?

"Don't you worry, my dear," suggested the Marquis gently. "We'll think of something."

"What?" she asked desperately.

"For the moment, I don't know," he had to admit.

There came a loud knock on the door and peeping through the window, Madame Ducros gave a little cry.

"It's an Officer in naval uniform."

"Let him enter," called out Pierre heroically. "I am ready. But my sweet Felicity, kiss me once more and say you will wait for me."

"*Forever,*" she declared wildly.

Monsieur Ducros then opened the door, admitting the Officer. He looked very large and very intimidating as he approached Pierre.

"Pierre Ducros?" he demanded in a stern voice.

Pierre stood to attention.

"I am he."

The Officer pulled something out of his coat.

"Here are all your papers. In the rush you dropped them this morning. I tried to call you back to give them to you, but you went too quickly. I wish you every happiness with this pretty lady. Good day to you all."

He gave an elegant bow to the ladies and departed.

There was total pandemonium. The sudden relief and happiness sent everyone wild.

Father Bernard now examined Pierre's passport and nodded. Since the wedding had been arranged in advance, it could take place at once.

"It sounds like an excellent idea," said the Marquis. "It cannot be soon enough for me."

A few minutes later they joined the family in the little Church to witness the marriage of Pierre Ducros and Lady Felicity Wendover.

Then they descended on a nearby tavern along with a large crowd of friends and relatives to celebrate at the Marquis's expense.

There was music and dancing and the high point of the party was when Pierre extended his hand to his bride. Everyone else cleared the floor and they danced alone.

Now Selina saw what the Marquis had meant about Felicity's dancing. As she dipped and swayed elegantly in Pierre's arms, it was clear that this was her real talent.

Her thinking might often be brainless, but when she communicated through movement she conveyed thoughts and feelings with great intensity.

When they had finished there was loud applause.

"We'll be going on the stage," Felicity announced when they returned to the table. "We'll travel around the country performing engagements wherever we can."

It might sound an outrageous ambition for a girl of her background, but Selina was seeing her anew.

Felicity was wasted as a Duke's daughter. She was a true artiste and had chosen her path. Her eyes were now shining with joy and fulfilment.

"We're going to be a great success," she enthused. "I just know it."

"And I know it too," beamed the Marquis. "You'll be a success because the two of you just cannot fail. When you've found the person that you can love more than all the world, then you can face anything together."

"It will happen for you too," Felicity told him.

"Perhaps," he murmured. "I don't know – *but I live in hope.*"

He did not look at Selina as he spoke and it seemed to her that he was deliberately avoiding her eyes.

"But surely," he then continued, "you should have a honeymoon first? I would suggest that you take my yacht and head off to the Mediterranean for a month or two."

The merry party descended on the yacht, where he gave instructions to the Captain and arranged to have his possessions and Selina's taken ashore.

They stood together on the quayside watching *The Mermaid* sail away, waving at the newly-weds in the stern waving back to them.

"Well!" sighed Selina. "What now?"

The Marquis turned to the driver of the carriage as he was stowing their bags in the hold.

"Take us to the best hotel in town," he ordered.

# CHAPTER TEN

The Marquis took two suites at *The Imperial Hotel*.

When an army of servants had carried their bags up they each retreated to the joys of hot baths before meeting again for a meal in the evening.

That evening Selina took infinite trouble with her appearance, donning an elegant gown and putting her hair up.

Yet he barely seemed to notice. His compliment was almost mechanical.

She found him in a strange mood – almost skittish, she would have said of anyone else. Instead of going over their future plans, as she had hoped, he seemed to shy away from any kind of serious talk.

He would begin to discuss something, then abandon it half way through, so that it was impossible for her mind to take a firm hold on what he was saying – if indeed he was really trying to say anything at all.

"Selina," he enquired, "have you ever stood at a crossroads to find that each road looked equally inviting, but you knew that one would take you where you wanted to go and one would make a complete mess of everything?

"But you couldn't tell which one was which, and you thought, if only you could foresee the future, except that you can't because life doesn't make it that easy – "

He broke off, alarmed by the way she was staring at him.

"I'm gibbering nonsense, aren't I?"

"Worse. You are beginning to sound like Felicity!"

"Am I? Good Heavens! Then I must stop."

For the rest of the meal he told her amusing stories, and when they retired to bed, she was no nearer seeing into his mind than she had ever been.

But a good sleep restored her spirits and when she rose she was once more full of hope.

Having dressed, she looked out of the window and breathed in the sea air wondering just where this wonderful adventure would take her next.

Below a carriage was rumbling up to the hotel door. She watched idly as the two occupants climbed out.

Then she froze in horror as she saw who they were.

In a moment she was out of her room and running to the Marquis's suite, knocking frantically on his door.

He opened it at once.

"Selina, what's happened? Is the hotel on fire?"

"Much worse," she gasped loudly. "*They* are here. The Duke and my stepfather. I've just seen them get out of a carriage in front of the hotel."

"Ah!" he muttered.

"*Ah*?" she echoed. "Is that all you can say?"

He drew her inside and closed the door.

"We always knew that this moment was bound to come sooner or later. We couldn't go on running for ever. It'll be rather interesting to see Wendover's face when he realises that he has lost."

"Do we have to stay here and see it? Cannot we leave before they find us?"

"I don't really think that anything can to be gained by that," he said reflectively. "It would be much better to sort everything out now – once and for all."

Horrified, it dawned on her what he might mean.

He had grown bored with this adventure and now that he was safe from having to marry Felicity, he had no further interest in helping her.

And yet everything inside her cried out against the accusation. The Marquis, the man she had come to know and love, could never be guilty of such baseness.

But how well did she really know him?

As though he had read her thoughts, he said gently,

"Selina, I have asked you to trust me in the past and you have always said that you do. Can you go on trusting me just a little longer, even if I seem to behave strangely?"

Suddenly she was calm.

She put her hands into his.

"Of course, Ian, I trust you, completely."

"In everything?"

"With my life and beyond."

"Then we might manage this venture successfully."

"Cannot you tell me what you're going to do?"

"It's best if you don't know. But I think – yes, I'm sure – that the time has come for me to be unassertive."

"Surely you mean assertive?" Selina asked, startled.

A light that might just have been mischief gleamed in his eyes.

"Oh no, my dear, that isn't what I mean at all. In fact, I sometimes think a man may gain more from being a milksop than he ever would from bawling his head off."

"A *milksop*?" she repeated in bewilderment.

"Would you be very ashamed of me, if I acted like a milksop, Selina?"

His voice was apologetic, almost meek, but Selina could sense that things were not all they seemed.

Despite his words there seemed a reckless air about him she had not seen before. He looked like a man who was about to chance everything on one throw of the dice.

"You're planning something, aren't you? You are no more a milksop than – than I am."

"I'm very glad you know. But keep the knowledge to yourself for a while or you'll spoil my effect."

Before she could say more they heard the sound of angry bellowing coming from the far end of the corridor.

Selina could detect the brash voice of her stepfather and it made her feel ill.

"They're coming," she whispered to the Marquis. "Oh, Heavens, he'll drag me away."

"No he won't."

The next moment the door was flung open and the man she had dreaded to see stood on the threshold.

John Gardner's eyes gleamed at the sight of her.

"So there you are, my girl! Thought you could get away from me, did you? Well, you'll find out differently. Come here."

"One moment," snapped the Duke. "I have business of my own. You sir – " he pointed at the Marquis. "You have deceived me. You told me you were engaged to this lady, but I am reliably informed that it's not true. She is already engaged, although she does not act like it."

"Because I am *not* –" stated Selina, as firmly as she could manage.

"That is for me to say," interrupted John Gardner dangerously.

"No, it's for *me* to say," she flashed at him. "And I say it's not true."

"Now look here, my girl – "

"*Silence!*" roared the Duke, bawling straight into his face. "Keep your petty concerns until I am finished."

It had been years since anyone had dared to speak to John Gardner like this. But he was a Duke and his awe of 'the quality' was so great that he fell silent.

"Now you," the Duke yelled at the Marquis, "you'll not play fast and loose with me again. You'll marry my daughter or, by God, I'll know the reason why."

"But I am more than happy to tell you the reason why," retorted the Marquis plaintively. "I cannot marry your daughter, as she is already married."

"No more of your tricks – "

"No tricks, I swear it. She was married yesterday in a Church near here. Lady Selina and I were witnesses and the happy couple left for England on the evening tide."

The Duke eyed him, his face turning an ugly grey.

"You are bluffing," he declared. "I demand to see my daughter at once. What have you done with her, sir?"

"What have I done with her?" the Marquis echoed vaguely. "Well, let me see, I put her aboard my yacht, and her husband of course. I wished them both a safe journey, and watched them sail away."

The Duke seemed about to explode.

"And just who is this husband?" he demanded.

"I believe his name is Pierre Ducros."

"What?" roared the Duke. "That dreadful wastrel, that scoundrel? How dare you help her to marry him?"

"My dear sir, it is no business of mine whom your daughter marries. I can assure you that she did not want to marry me."

"I just don't believe it," blustered the Duke. "It's a trick to throw me off the scent."

143

But his voice had lost its vigour.

"My dearest daughter," he coughed hoarsely. "My daughter – married to a dancer!"

"But to a man who loves her," the Marquis pointed out. "Surely that must make you glad?"

The Duke flung him a look of loathing.

"You think you've been clever, making a fool of me," he snapped. "But I'll have the last laugh. You've left yourself exposed, Castleton."

"Exposed? To what?"

"To *him*," he screamed, indicating John Gardner. "I've travelled in his company these last few days and a more vulgar, stupid, ignorant blockhead I have yet to meet! You'll be lucky if you don't end up with him for a father-in-law."

Selina tensed in an agony of embarrassment.

What would the Marquis think of her?

But he hardly seemed to register the significance of the words.

"Oh no," he muttered rather vaguely. "Gardner is selling Lady Selina to pay off his debts."

Selina's gasp was audible.

John Gardner blenched.

"You'll take that back," he snarled.

"No, I don't think I will. You do owe Ralph Turner money, don't you? That's why he can demand from you whatever he likes. The Captain of my yacht hears all the rumours in Portsmouth and he gave me a pretty good idea of what you owe this man.

"Then it all began to make sense. If you were one tenth as wealthy as you make out, you would be seeking to achieve your social ambitions in quite another way. A title like mine would be out of your league, of course. No man with a title would look at you for a moment, but I suppose you might have snared a Baronet!"

Never had Selina heard him speak with such lofty discourteous superiority. Was this what he called being unassertive?

But she said nothing. It was clear that he was up to something that she did not understand.

The Marquis sighed.

"Actually your so-called wealth is no more than a sham. One touch would bring you crashing down."

Having delivered this devastating snub, he yawned.

John Gardner's face turned to a ghastly colour and Selina could not doubt that the accusation was true.

Everything about him was a fraud. He had tried to sell her.

And with that thought the last chain seemed to fall from her.

She was free of him.

It was a strange, poverty-stricken kind of freedom, but she would make something of it.

"I think you should leave now," she told him. "We have nothing more to say to each other."

"You just don't understand," he croaked hoarsely, "if you don't come back, I am ruined. All right, perhaps I did some things the wrong way, but I've always been good to you. You owe me something."

"I owe you *nothing*. You were good to yourself."

"I impoverished myself providing your mother with a comfortable life," he yelped.

"For your own reasons and your own gain and then you tried to barter me like an animal you owned. After that I have no sense of obligation to you.

"Besides," she added thoughtfully, "Ralph Turner will not want me when he learns about this journey. He'll think it most improper. I am sure his money can buy him something better than me."

"No, no, he must never know about this," Gardner gibbered.

Selina looked him in the eye.

"I shall personally make sure that he knows about everything."

The Marquis swung round on her.

"My dear Selina!" he exclaimed, apparently totally horrified. "Everything?"

"Everything," she asserted firmly.

"Including – " he muttered, "Cedric Ponsonby?"

"Even him."

"Who's he?" Gardner bawled. "How many men have you – ?"

"Does it matter?" asked the Marquis. "Especially after the night at that post house at Picthaven."

"What?" gasped Gardner.

"It was the inn's fault," the Marquis explained. "I reserved two separate rooms, but there was a mix-up. Of course, I would never have mentioned this myself, being a gentleman, but since Lady Selina is determined to reveal all to a censorious world – "

He gave an elegant shrug.

"She wouldn't dare!" howled John Gardner

"Why not?" demanded Selina. "What do I have to lose?"

"Your reputation."

"After this journey, how much reputation do I have left?" she countered lightly.

She was almost enjoying herself. Later there would be huge problems, she realised. The life of a free woman would not be easy. But for the moment, all she could feel was the exhilaration of casting her shackles aside.

John Gardner had not given up.

As he saw ruin facing him, he became more frantic and unreasonable.

"You'll think better of it when you've seen sense," he spluttered. "You'll keep quiet and I'll keep quiet, and not a word of this will ever get out – "

"But, of course, it will," interrupted the Marquis. "You are just forgetting that Wendover, here, has a grudge against Lady Selina for helping me to thwart him. He'll ensure that the story of our journey is known everywhere."

The sneer on the Duke's face bore him out.

"Then I'm no further use to you," Selina told John Gardner. "And I'm free of you *at last*."

"You think it will be just that easy?" he fumed. "A ruined woman, that's what you'll be! See if anyone wants to know you, because *he* – " he shot out his right arm at the Marquis who was observing the scene with elaborate lack of concern, "*he* won't marry you. You're not good enough for him. You heard him say so."

"Actually," the Marquis retorted, "what I said was that *you* were not good enough. The lady herself is the equal of any man."

He smiled as he added,

"It's just that she is unfortunate in her relatives."

Having thoroughly insulted Gardner, he turned his back on him.

"Now, you look here! Don't think you can take this attitude with me."

"My dear fellow, what is to stop me?" the Marquis mumbled over his shoulder, sounding bored.

"How you can stand there, so free and easy, when you've ruined an innocent girl – ?"

"It's exactly what he did to *my* daughter," the Duke observed. "If I couldn't move him, what chance do you think you'll have?"

"I'll complain to the Queen," Gardner bellowed.

The Marquis turned back.

"And what, exactly, do you plan to say about me?"

"That you're a scoundrel and a blackguard and you owe it to this girl to make an honest woman of her."

The Marquis regarded Selina curiously.

"Would it make you happy to marry a scoundrel and a blackguard?" he asked her.

"Certainly not," she answered at once. "Besides, you don't owe me anything."

"But Mr. Gardner seems to think I've ruined you."

"Mr. Gardner knows nothing about the matter. I intend to make my name as an author, starting with a book about my recent experiences."

"Would it feature me, by any chance?" the Marquis asked nervously.

"Naturally, but so heavily disguised that no one will know that it's you. So you see, there is no need for you to marry me. In fact you would be much wiser not to."

"There you are," the Marquis told John Gardner. "The matter is settled."

"It most certainly is not," seethed Gardner. "Are you going to listen to a silly girl who knows nothing of the world? I demand that you do the honourable thing and marry her!"

The Marquis looked nonplussed.

"Do you?"

"I insist upon it."

The Marquis scratched his head.

"I see. Well then, I seem to have no choice."

"What?" Selina stared at him. "You cannot mean it. Don't just give in to him. Can't you see what he's up to? He thinks he'll get his claws into you now. He has it all worked out that you'll save him from ruin."

"Well, I suppose I will have to do *something*."

"Don't let him batten on you," she begged.

"But you heard him. He insists on our marriage."

"But you don't have to listen to him," she urged.

"Well – don't you think I should? I suppose, in the circumstances – "

"You mean to make an honest woman of me?" she demanded, incensed. "Well, perhaps I have some thoughts about that myself."

The flicker of a smile crossed his face.

"It would greatly surprise me if you didn't. But I do hope you won't refuse me out of prejudice."

"Prejudice?" roared John Gardner. "You think any female is going to turn down such a chance? You thank your lucky stars, my girl, that I've whipped him into line for you. You could have been abandoned if I hadn't taken a strong stand."

"Yes," murmured the Marquis. "It's so lucky I'm such a milksop, isn't it?"

Looking in his eyes Selina understood everything, including why he had played this scene the way he had.

And yet something stubbornly independent in her could not leave matters there.

"I will *not* marry you, my Lord."

"My dear, I think you'll have to," he sighed. "Your stepfather is so determined that I am shaking in my shoes. You must say *yes* – for my sake!"

Selina now spoke through gritted teeth,

"Will you come into the next room with me? I do need to speak to you privately?"

He recoiled.

"Do I dare? If you are as fearsome as he is, I am afraid my nerves are not up to it."

"Then you would not want to marry a woman who would certainly bully you," she parried, her eyes glinting.

He smiled at her.

Selina tried to be serious, but it was hard when that teasing smile could make her heart turn over.

"Kindly oblige me by coming into the next room," she repeated.

He groaned.

"If I must, I must. I see I am condemned to live under the cat's paw."

"Will you stop talking nonsense?" she demanded wrathfully, opening the door and pulling him through it.

When she had shut the door firmly behind them she began to speak urgently.

"Ian, I understand what you are doing and it's very chivalrous of you, but truly there is no need. You must not marry me for such a reason and if you – "

She could say no more.

His arms went swiftly around her and the last words were cut off by a ruthless kiss. There was nothing of the milksop about his Lordship at *this* moment.

She gave a faint murmur, which might have been a protest at the ungentle way he was handling her, but his arms quickly tightened and his mouth crushed hers more determinedly, silencing her.

It was not their first kiss, but it was different from the other time in the storm. Then he had been fighting himself, desiring her but trying not to desire her.

Now it was the opposite.

Not only did he not want to deny his feelings, he was letting her know about them in the most unmistakable manner.

There was promise and intent in the way his lips caressed hers.

"Now," he murmured at last, "do you understand why I want to marry you?"

"I'm – not quite sure."

"Then I will have to explain it again."

This time it look longer and was as much her kiss as his.

Selina's head was spinning.

There were so many things she wanted to say, so many explanations that needed to be made before she could really make a decision about marrying him.

But somehow all the words were not important and the decision seemed to have already been made although she could not imagine when.

A long time ago perhaps in another world.

When he released her she clung on to him, feeling giddy.

"You made it happen, didn't you?" she whispered.

"My darling, I can be a most determined milksop when I set my mind to it. I've wanted to marry you almost

151

since the first moment, but I didn't know how to persuade you."

"Persuade me?"

"I've been so conscious that I am older than you – "

"Not that much older," she answered loyally.

"No, but I've always felt older than my years. You are so young and full of life and I am so dull and serious. And you plainly weren't interested in me."

"I wasn't – ?"

"I did attempt to ask you to marry me earlier, but it misfired."

"When?"

"After Simpkins's accident, when we were trying to decide how to go on together and you had the idea of being a boy. Do you remember that I had another idea?"

"You were trying to propose to me, *then*?"

"Yes, for a wild moment I thought I could get you to marry me to save your reputation, but you never even heard what I was trying to say.

"Then, I thought, perhaps you did hear me and had pretended not to, just to put me off. Either way, it was clear you didn't see me as a husband and afterwards I was glad it didn't happen like that.

"I would always have wondered why you had said yes and if you cared about me as much as I loved you."

"If I – ? Oh Ian, I was falling in love with you, but I thought that you were just doing what you felt to be your duty. You always promised that you would behave like a perfect gentleman."

"Of course. I owed it to you not to take advantage of your vulnerability."

He looked at her more closely.

"What are you saying? That you didn't want me to keep that promise?"

"There were times when I wouldn't have minded if you had broken it just a little," she admitted.

"My darling!"

"But you seemed to manage it so easily – "

"Easily? If you only knew, Selina, I have wanted so much to tell you of my feelings, but I was afraid to, and that you would see me as a burden and were trying not to compromise me so you could escape.

"Well, I compromised you very thoroughly in there, didn't I? You have to marry me now. I am afraid I've left you no escape route. Forgive me. I'll spend the rest of my life making sure that you never regret our marriage.

"My darling, my darling, come here! I am about to forget that I am a gentleman again!"

For the next few minutes he forgot it thoroughly.

Selina gladly gave herself up to his many wild and passionate kisses, meeting his desire with hers whilst her heart sang.

"Now I want your answer, Selina. Will you marry me?"

"With all my heart. I want to spend the rest of my life with you. But, oh, my love, how my stepfather will gloat over you."

"Let him, just as long as he grants me what I really need, which is you?"

"I think I understand why you did it that way," she said uncertainly. "But I was puzzled sometimes."

"I knew from what you had already told me that, in John Gardner, I was dealing with a bully. And the most certain method of defeating a bully is to let him think he is forcing you to do what you actually want to do.

"If I'd asked for your hand he would have opposed me to the last breath in his body out of spite for spoiling his plans with Turner. He is quite stupid enough to do that without thinking, even against his own interests.

"Now he's surely congratulating himself on getting the better of me, so I don't think we will have any further trouble with him.

"Just the same, I think we will marry quickly, right here. If we wait to return to England, he might start being difficult and I am not going to risk it."

"Nor am I. But darling – " a thought struck her, "About England, I thought Felicity and Pierre are sailing on to the Mediterranean."

"They are."

"But you told the Duke they're going to England."

"Did I? Are you sure that is what I said?"

Her lips twitched.

"Positive."

"Oh, dear, how very remiss of me. My memory is becoming shocking these days."

"You could hardly have forgotten that."

"I can forget anything at all if I set my mind to it," he declared firmly. "Never mind, the Duke will discover my mistake eventually – "

"When he's chased them to England and discovered that they're not there!" she supplied.

"I daresay. Let's forget them. I'll apologise for my 'mistake' another time."

"The Duke will gloat over you too, having to accept my Mr. Gardner as a father-in-law."

The Marquis shrugged.

"If I have you, I can cope with any number of John Gardners!"

He put his ear to the door and Selina joined him.

From the other side came the sound of altercation.

"They're at it hammer and tongs. It is worse than Martha and Simpkins and I feel rather disinclined to rejoin them."

"But what else can we do?"

The Marquis grinned.

"This."

He began pulling his papers and money out of the drawer where he kept his valuables. Then he threw a few overnight things into a bag.

"We'll send for the rest later."

"Ian, you don't mean – ?"

He placed a finger over his lips, took her hand and led her to the door. They slipped into the corridor and then moved quietly past the main door to his suite from behind which they could still hear angry voices.

The Duke and John Gardner were both deep in the business of blaming each other

"Now, your things, Selina."

In her suite she packed her bag speedily and then they were off, moving down the grand staircase.

In the lobby the Marquis next approached the major domo.

"Which is the next best hotel in Le Havre?"

"The second best hotel, my Lord, is our sister hotel, *The Majestic*, just a mile away."

"Then that is just where we are going. This money should more than cover the bill here. Keep the change, please have our luggage sent on to *The Majestic*, but on no account reveal to anyone – anyone at all – where we are."

He took Selina's hand and they ran into the street, hailing a passing cab.

"But surely we cannot do this," she protested when they were inside and the cab was moving.

"We've just done it."

"But – just to leave them like that – waiting for us to return – "

"Eventually they'll realise that we aren't going to. But it'll probably take them some time, the way they were going at it."

She began to laugh and he joined in.

They clasped each other and sang out their joy in peal after peal, until the Marquis pulled her closer and the laughter stopped.

The cab rumbled away down the street, taking them to their new life of unbridled happiness.

Selina could think of nothing but the Marquis – his lips, his arms and the fire of love rising like burning flames within them both.

Their hearts beat to the music of love, the stars fell down from the sky to cover them with stardust and angels carried them to a special Heaven where there was only real love that would envelop them for all Eternity.

Meanwhile in the hotel two selfish and thwarted men continued to argue and fight, not knowing that they had been left behind.

They are probably arguing still.